CONNECT THE DOTS

A Forked Tongue Press Anthology
Of Horror Stories

A FORKED TONGUE BOOK

November 2007

Published by

Forked Tongue Press
Baltimore, MD
United States

ISBN-13: 978-0-6151-8408-1

Printed in the United States of America

CONTENTS

CONNECT
THE
DOTS

CONNECT THE DOTS
(Part one)
By Alexzan Burton

Penetrate the flesh
Extract the soul
Our words like liquid life

Like liquid strife
It is suffering...

The demons in the heads
Of the writers
Of visionary confinement

Open our veins
And in the blood
Spattered on the walls,

Connect the dots.

WHEN THE LIGHTNING FLASHES
By Gregory L Hall

My name is Linnea. And mine is a victim's story. I'm sole witness of a horrific tragedy. I'm trying hard to learn why some people are chosen to be survivors while their family and friends aren't so lucky. So many memories of that night I've been able to block away. Buried deep where they can't hurt me anymore. But so many others still haunt me in my sleep.

These people all come around to ask me the gory details, about the blood bath, about how it all happened. Some are even stupid enough to ask me how I feel about it. How do I feel? Can you imagine such an idiotic question? Everyone I ever loved was slaughtered. How do you think I feel?

Well, I'm sure you want to hear my story just like all the others. I guess there's always going to be some sort of morbid fascination. To watch 'Friday the 13th' or 'Halloween' is one thing. To talk with someone who actually lived through the same horror in real life? I guess I can understand.

I'd be curious myself if it hadn't happened to me.

October in Maryland. A beautiful time of year in our beautiful neighborhood. Things were just settling in for the Fall. The leaves were finally turning colors and we'd rake them up from our nice lawns. School was in full swing. Weekends were spent supporting local football. I grew up here. Everybody knew everybody. Life was happy.

It was a Thursday night. I was watching the lightning flashing outside. No storm. Just lightning. Couldn't even hear the thunder. It was like God's fireworks. I pulled a blanket out of our cedar chest and slouched down on the couch. My brother Danny was in the kitchen, trying to be cute with my mother on the phone. It was a rare night out for them. Mom and Dad were celebrating with a few friends. Some kind of job promotion Dad got. Adults eating steak dinners and drinking all night. My brother and I weren't invited.

"Everything is fine, Mom. Stop worrying. We're big kids now. Well, at least I am."

We exchanged looks of sibling hatred.

"No, I haven't seen Tuck all night. I think the stupid dog ran off. Probably getting laid… No, I said 'he needs to be spade.' Jesus, Mom."

Danny always thought he was so clever. I let him know I would correct that situation when Mom got home. He gave me the finger.

"I love you too, Mom. We're okay, honest. You and Dad stay out and have fun. Seriously. We ordered pizza. Yes. I already said I love you. Sheesh!"

Danny hung up the phone and plopped down next to me on the couch. He snatched the bowl of popcorn from my lap and started shoving it into his face.

"I wanted to talk to Mom and Dad."

"They didn't want to talk to you. They had to go. I think Mom was calling from the back seat of the SUV. I could hear Dad breathing heavy."

"You're so gross."

"Facts of life. How do you think they made you?"

The lightning flashed and the electricity went out for a second. For the first time, I heard the thunder. It made me feel uncomfortable.

"Wow. Pretty scary. Reminds me of that story about the killer who used to live in this neighborhood." Big brother stared straight into my eyes. "The ax murderer."

"You're not funny, Danny."

"I'm not joking. You were just a little kid. You wouldn't remember, but it was all over the place. Made national news. He went into a mental institution but escaped. The cops never talk about it because they have no idea where he disappeared to. But they say on nights like this, when the lightning flashes, he could appear again. And that would be the last thing his victims would ever see."

Lightning lit up the living room and Danny grabbed my arm. I screamed. Popcorn flew everywhere and he laughed his ass off.

"I'm not cleaning that up, you asshole!" I punched him as hard as I could but he didn't care. He stomped on the popcorn and went back into the kitchen again. "I hate you, Danny!"

"Well, you better learn to love me. Mom said some of Dad's business buddies showed up late so they're going to be staying out for quite awhile. And they put me in charge." Danny pointed to himself and then to me. He couldn't be more condescending."Senior. freshman. Remember that."

He opened the basement door. I sat up.

"Where are you going?"

"Down into the spooky old basement. To get some of Dad's beers. And don't think about telling or Mom will find out about your little love fests with Chris Brandon next door."

"Liar! What did Chris tell you about the shed?"

"Nothing. But you just did!"

He gave me this ridiculous six-shooter gesture and disappeared into the basement.

God how I hated him.

I sat by myself for what seemed like forever. The silence was the type that was so quiet, your ears actually rang. I'm sure smart doctors would call it paranoia. I called it plain old scared shitless. And the worst part was I knew Danny was just waiting downstairs in the dark, ready to jump out and make me wet myself. And he knew I knew. So it was a test of wills.

I turned on the TV. I found 'Everybody Loves Raymond' within three clicks. Funny happy show. Real family comedy. And I thought Patricia Heaton was so pretty. Danny could sit in the basement with his stupid beer all night for all I cared.

The lightning hit right outside our bay window and everything went black. Raymond was gone.

"Danny?"

I pulled the blanket tight around my neck. I looked around and let my eyes adjust to the darkness. I thought I saw the basement door slowly swing open. And it sounded like someone was whispering.

I got up and cautiously moved towards the kitchen. The lightning flashed again and the entire room lit up. The basement door *was* open. And there was definitely whispering. Danny was probably trying to find his way back up the stairs in the dark.

"Danny? I'm coming into the kitchen so just come back upstairs now. Follow my voice. All the electricity is out."

No answer.

I wasn't staying upstairs alone. I didn't care if Danny scared the crap out of me. At least I'd know he was next to me. I opened the basement door all the way hoping to let what little light there might be guide me down the stairs. I was walking into complete darkness. My hands went to each wall trying to feel my way.

"Danny? Come on. Stop trying to scare me. Can you put the electricity back on? Please? Danny?"

I reached the bottom of the stairs in an awkward stumble off the last step. But I was there. I was okay. And my eyes were getting used to the dark. We had a few small windows near the top of the basement walls but they had thicker glass. Even in daytime, they didn't let very much light in. There was a back door that I could open and hopefully let some outside light into the back of the basement. And Dad's workbench was back there too. With his heavy utility flashlight in the furthest left-hand drawer. I paused briefly to get my bearings and then reached out for the closest wall.

I heard a foot drag across the concrete floor.

I froze in my position. My heart slammed against my ribs. Fear made my eyes grow wide to absorb every possible shape and obstacle around me. I moved again ever so slightly around the corner. I could make out the back door…because it was open. And dim light poured in. Around the outline of someone standing there. My voice cracked.

"Danny? Is that you?"

It didn't move.

Then out of the corner of my eye, I saw something fall to the floor beside me. It sounded like a wet bag or more accurately, heavy thick vomit splattering against the hard concrete. Fear won. I was going back upstairs. Quickly. I put my hand against the wall to find my way but I touched something warm, mushy, wet. The lightning flashed. I found Danny. He was hanging on the wall, his intestines sliding out of his torso.

The lightning flashed again and poured in from the outside doorway. I saw the silhouette clearly. An ax swinging in its hand.

I screamed and ran upstairs as fast as I could. I didn't even reach for the walls, just ran on memory and adrenaline. I tripped at the top of the stairs but my arms instantly caught me and I was back up again. I looked back behind me. The figure was barely illuminated down at the bottom of the steps, but I could see him. Casually swinging the ax back and forth.

The kitchen door was the closest way out and I knew exactly where it was. I could beat whoever was down in the basement across the back yard before they ever found their way upstairs. So I hit it running, jumped from the porch to the grass and didn't look back. I think I actually hurtled the fence at our property line. Only then did my brain stop to grasp the spinning world around me.

No one was following. God help me, Danny had better have pulled off the prank of the century. If this was some kind of joke, I was going to kill him for real. Chris lived two houses down. Danny wasn't going to be laughing so hard when I called the cops.

The air seemed a bit colder than it was only an hour before. And the storm still hadn't produced any rain. Just long weird clouds that hung low to the horizon. Small flashes within them made them glow dark purple. But at least the big bolts weren't hitting around the neighborhood for the time being.

The electricity was off everywhere so I moved to the middle of the street. I could see Chris' front porch as clear as day. I felt safer already.

I knocked on his door. And it swung open. I don't know if it was fear or simply good manners but I didn't enter.

"Chris? Mr., Mrs. Brandon? Anybody home?"

They had candles lit in their kitchen, one room back. And some more down the hallway to where the bathroom and bedrooms were. Their house was from the same model ours was. I stepped inside. My eyes scanned the living room and were able to make out Mr. Brandon sitting in his big padded Dad chair.

"Mr. Brandon? Is Chris here?"

One more step inside and something swished under my foot. I looked down just as the lightning crashed outside the open door. Mrs. Brandon was on the couch beside me. Her head in her lap. Mr. Brandon sat straight in his blood soaked Dad chair, his throat slashed wide open. And I was standing inside of Chris. His head rolled across the carpet and stopped against the entertainment center.

I didn't have time to scream. The kitchen door flew open in the wind. And the figure stepped inside.

I ran. Didn't know where I was going but I ran as fast and hard as I could. Headed back to the only safe place I knew. My house. I hopped the fence and landed near our shed. Instinct grabbed me and threw me inside the wooden door. I slid the metal bolt across the latch and backed my way in deeper, past the lawn mower and the inflatable pool gear. Moving towards the work bench and the tools. Never taking my eyes off the door.

My fingers scrambled wildly across the table top. Lawn shears. Screw driver. Sharp digging claw. Maybe even a knife. I needed a weapon.

The lightning flashed again and I automatically spun around to look out the only window in the entire shed. But all I saw was his face. Unshaven. Dirty greasy hair hanging into his eyes. His cold grey lifeless eyes.

I know I screamed. I know because I felt my throat rip until it was raw. I know I ran. I know because my legs felt like lead and my ankle throbbed. But I don't know when I hurt it, twisted it. And I don't know how I got from that shed into my own room. I only know I did.

I locked my bedroom door. I built a barricade. Pushed my full dresser against it. A chair. My laundry bin. I grabbed the phone. Dead. And our cell was downstairs on the kitchen counter. I wedged myself into the far corner of the room. I saw wild strikes of electricity light up the night sky in the distance.

The window. I was two stories up. Did I hear something against the outside wall? I couldn't be sure anymore. Couldn't trust my own senses. I wasn't going to take any chances. A ladder? The rainspout? Maybe up and over the roof from the deck out back? He'd find a way in.

My desk. I locked down the window and slid my desk in front of it. Turned it over on its side. I frantically pulled the blinds shut. Blocked out the light. Then crouched down and moved back to my corner. I lost all track of time. I heard the grandfather clock in the downstairs hallway. I counted the deep bongs. Actually bong. There was only one. And then the silence was overpowering. 1AM. Sunrise was a lifetime away. I let the darkness swallow me up.

I was slightly surprised when I awoke from my sleep. The sun had risen, illuminating my room in a comforting glow. The topsy-turvy desk in front of the window couldn't prevent the warm rays from entering. My eyes immediately surveyed the rest of the room. My other barricade was untouched. The door secure. My room was safe. The storm was gone. And I was still alive.

I had to physically pull myself from the crevice I had shoved myself into. My neck was sore. My shoulders stiff. My ankle still throbbed. I wondered if…

I heard my mother call upstairs. The sweetest voice I had ever heard.

"Linnea! Breakfast is ready! Wake up, sleepy head!"

I was confused. But absolute elation washed away my doubts. Mom was home. Like always. After a night out with Dad. He would be downstairs already at the kitchen table. I could almost smell the bacon. The hash brown potatoes. Breakfast was cooking.

But if that was true, then what of the horrible nightmare? Had they not been down to the basement yet? Did the killer hide Danny's body? Did they think he was still sleeping too? Was the killer still in the house somewhere? Or in the neighborhood waiting for night to fall again? Where was he? How could Mom and Dad not know?

Was I going crazy?

"Linnea, come on down! Your breakfast is going to get cold!"

I jumped up and shoved everything out of the way. I didn't care if I was nuts or not. I made it. I was going to be okay. Any way you wanted to paint it, the nightmare was over.

I ran out into the hallway. And tripped. I lifted my hand up and found it covered in blood. *I* was covered in blood. A huge pool of it.

"Your breakfast is getting cold…" my mother's voice deepened until it sounded like some demonic rambling. "….Everything is getting so cold."

My parents were butchered across the hallway floor. I heaved and added to the grotesque stench. Then he joined me. Right in the pool of blood. On all fours like a rabid wolf. His face mere inches from mine.

He smiled with cracked yellow teeth. I inhaled his rancid thick breath. And I hurled myself across the floor. Slid my flattened body through the blood until I was on the other side of my bedroom door. I felt the whoosh of the ax blade over my head a second before I slammed the door shut. I heard his raspy whisper seep through the cracks.

"Linnea…"

I could see his shadow bounce back and forth underneath the door. I threw the dresser back in his path. He kicked at the door. I flung the chair into the pile. His fists beat on the door and it opened. I shoved back and secured the lock. His voice grew into a roar that shook my whole room.

"Linnea! Linnea-Linnea-Linnea!"

I flew backwards and crammed myself into my tight corner. The door buckled and cracked. I screamed. The lock burst and fingers frantically stretched inside. My lungs emptied themselves of all air. The barricade toppled over and the figure forced itself through the thin opening.

"And that's when the police found you?"

"Yes."

"Covered in blood. And still holding the ax in your hand?"

Linnea looked up at the psychiatrist and smiled. The restraints on her wrists made her feel safe. Her voice was deep, with no remorse, as she recited her answer like some twisted children's rhyme.

"Isn't it strange when the lightning flashes the only one left standing is you?"

THE END

Outside In
By Jezzy Wolfe

It was no accident.

The body lay twisted in a crumpled heap, appendages twisted in angles that were impossible to mimic. Both arms and legs were fractured, and the head was busted open. Her eyes stared vacantly at the ceiling. Lacey stared at her for what felt like an eternity, even though she knew the shattered victim could never be healed.

"Dammit, Ellie, why do you have to be such a brat?" Lacey wheeled on her younger sister, who had planted herself obstinately behind her, both feet cemented to the worn carpet of the stairwell landing. "Granny gave me that doll right before she died! Why'd ya hafta throw it?"

"You're supposed to share! Mom said!" Ellie's bottom lip stuck out petulantly, and Lacey fought the urge to back hand her.

"That was not a toy, you little shithead! Now she's ruined!"

"I don't care! And I'm telling Momma you cursed at me. You're gonna be in big trouble when she gets home!" Ellie pushed her big sister aside and scrambled down the stairs. When she reached the bottom she glared up at Lacey. Their eyes clashed for a second, and then a twisted smile crossed Ellie's small face, contorting her features into something monstrous. As Lacey watched, she lifted her left foot and stomped on the remnants of Lacey's ceramic doll, pulverizing the jagged pieces to dust.

Ellie's laughter trailed behind as she skipped off to some other part of the house, but Lacey didn't bother chasing after her. She slumped onto the bottom step and fingered the busted bits of her doll.

Truthfully, she wasn't as angry as she was resigned. Ellie's behavior was an ever worsening condition that the family had simply grown accustomed to over the past five years. They had battled it with therapy and medications, but she continually grew more resilient. And resentful. Dr. Beakins told them it would be hard to reform Ellie's bad temper if they didn't understand where her anger stemmed from, but no one had any logical answers. Her behavior had been spiraling out of control long before their father died.

Since they had moved into their aunt's house, Ellie had become completely uncontrollable.

The sound of shattering glass broke Lacey's reverie, and she bolted in the direction of the cries, her heart pounding so hard she could barely hear her sister's wails. She found Ellie in the kitchen, her small fists balled in front of her, thick red drops seeping through her fingers and puddling on the linoleum. One of the glass panes of the back door speckled the floor around Ellie's feet, but Lacey was too distracted by Ellie's blood to ask what had happened. She snatched a dishtowel from a nearby counter and pushed Ellie into a chair, trying to pry open her clenched hands. "Come on; let me see 'em. I promise I won't hurt you."

Ellie relaxed her fingers slowly, revealing palms painted bloody by large gashes that extended across both hands. Despite wiggling protests, Lacey managed to dab away enough of the blood to see that the cuts weren't deep. She led her sister to the sink, and slowly ran warm water over her wounds, before wrapping clean towels around each hand. Ellie had stopped trembling and grew silent, but her eyes were wide and fearful.

"Okay, wanna tell me what happened? How did you break the window?" Lacey was careful not to sound too angry. At the moment, she kinda felt sorry for the little monster.

"I didn't do it, Lacey. She did."

Lacey groaned and rolled her eyes. Not this again. Ellie's conveniently invisible friend had obviously come to play. "Get off it Ellie, I ain't stupid. There's no one here but us. Tell me what really happened?"

"I'm not lyin! She was here when I came in the kitchen. I told her I couldn't play, and she got mad and broke the window. She did it just to get me in trouble!" She was trembling again, and Lacey could see the beginnings of another tantrum, so she relented.

"Okay, okay. Fine. Whatever you say. But Aunt Francine is gonna be pissed when she sees what happened to the back door." As Ellie watched, Lacey fetched the broom and swept the shards of glass into a pile, and then grabbed a wad of wet paper towels to wipe out the puddle of blood. Once again annoyed, she scowled up at her sister. "Can't you help? It's your mess. Get the dustpan and sweep up the glass."

"No." Pulling her shoulders back, she studied Lacey as if she were sizing up the opposition. "I'm not gonna."

Lacey lost the remains of her patience. "Quit being a little ass and help me!"

"Do it yourself, bitch."

Lacey was too shocked to respond. Certainly Ellie was more than an unpleasant handful, but she had never once used such foul language during any of their clashes. It hadn't even sounded like her- not really. Wasn't so much what she said, but how she said it. The nasally whine of a spoiled brat had been replaced by a voice cold and emotionless. Lacey stared dumbfounded as the girl sauntered out of the room, before returning to her task with shaking hands. Uneasy, she retreated to the safety of her bedroom for the remainder of the evening.

Two days passed without event, and Ellie was unusually complacent, if not downright polite. Lacey braced herself for Ellie's wrath repeatedly, but the usual conflicts failed to trigger Ellie's inner demon. Even when Lacey barked at her for hogging the television remote, Ellie would meekly apologize and abandon the television all together. Lacey would find her afterwards, often playing quietly with her dolls or coloring pictures.

Guilt was gnawing at Lacey over their previous argument. She was the closest thing to a friend or companion Ellie had. Their mom worked even more than necessary just to avoid her youngest child, and Lacey had also begun steering clear of her completely. Imagining how lonely she must feel, she sought Ellie out.

Aunt Francine's house was a dilapidated monolithic structure looming at the end of a cul-de-sac. They'd been there for nearly four months, but the girls were too intimidated to explore the third floor or the attic. If the overhead scuffles were any indication, the house was probably infested with rats the size of wombats, and neither were overly fond of the vermin. They squelched their usual nosiness and stayed away from all the closed doors and dark hallways. Ellie was particularly scared of crawling creatures, and slept with a nightlight glowing by her door to keep away any potential four-legged roomies.

Lacey was surprised to find Ellie's room vacant. Her first thought was that Ellie was snooping around in her bedroom, so she barged in abruptly, ready for battle. But Ellie wasn't there. She checked in her mother's bedroom, but once again, no Ellie. There was one other room, a spare room that Francine had used for storage, but Ellie wasn't there, either.

Thump!

Lacey nearly jumped out of her skin and bit back an oath. It sounded like someone dropped a bowling ball above her head. "Ellie?" Her response was thirty seconds of silence, followed by three more bumps. She didn't relish the idea of going upstairs, but she didn't know where else Ellie could be, and the thought occurred to her that Ellie might have gotten hurt. Mumbling worriedly under her breath, she stopped only momentarily before ascending the stairs to the third floor landing.

"Ellie?"

The corridor was dark, and Lacey wasn't sure how many rooms were up there. She felt along the walls for a switch plate, but either the light bulb was blown or the wiring was shot. Wishing she had brought a flashlight, she slowly crept through the hall, her hands gliding the walls in front of her. She passed a door on her right and then another on her left, but found no signs of life. "ELLIE!"

She heard the mischievous giggle of a young girl floating from one of the rooms ahead. Ellie's idea of a joke seriously failed to amuse her, and at that moment she was ready to strangle the girl within an inch of her life. A very faint shaft of light glowed from beneath a door at the far end of the hallway so she made her way through the dark as quick as possible and pushed into the room.

Dingy beige walls were illuminated by the lone lamp that sat isolated on a small desk. Scattered around the room were bits of clothing and discarded papers. To the far right a door stood open. Lacey tripped over an old pocket book to get to it, thinking perhaps Ellie was hiding in the closet. Instead, she found another staircase. Lacey backed away from the door, shivering. She did NOT want to go into the attic.

"Watch out. She's in a bad mood today." Ellie was sitting on the floor, combing the hair of a doll that looked about twenty five years old. She didn't look up to meet the stunned gaze of her sister; she was too focused on her toy. Lacey was certain she hadn't been there a minute before.

"She? You mean your doll?" Nervously, she lowered herself onto the floor by Ellie, never taking her eyes off the attic door.

"She told me I can play with it long as I'm nice to her." She pulled the doll's hair into a lopsided ponytail. "But if I'm not nice, she says she'll tell."

Lacey snorted and leaned against her sister, whispering, "Yeah, but it won't do her no good if nobody can hear her, will it?"

She expected Ellie's reply to be an impish grin.

She did not expect the grave expression on Ellie's face, or the solemn bow of her head. That was when Lacey noticed the two large bruises on her thigh, about an inch above her knee. It looked like she had been struck by a baseball. "Good God, Ellie, what happened?"

Ellie clutched the hem of her skirt and tried to pull it over her legs. Lacey caught another brief glimpse of deep purple. She seized Ellie's arm. A plum sized bruise covered her small forearm, and Lacey could see clearly eight deep burgundy crescents in the center. Teeth marks.

"Why are you biting yourself?" She tried remembering where her mom kept Dr. Beakins' number. It had been a few months since he'd seen Ellie, and her medication had run out a couple months back. About time for another visit, she decided.

"I was wearing her favorite dress and she got angry at me." The doll hopped in a circle and then turned a cartwheel. Lacey gently took the doll from her, hoping to get her full attention; however, Ellie grasped the doll with both hands and jerked it away. "You're not allowed to play with it. She said so."

Sighing in exasperation, Lacey pushed herself to her feet. "Who is she, Ellie? Since you refuse to fess up, does your invisible friend have a name yet?"

Ellie glared at her for the longest time without saying a word. Eventually, she dismissed her big sister by refocusing her attention on the doll. Lacey waited in silence for some acknowledgement, but Ellie was in a different world, crooning to the doll in low soothing tones.

"Fine. That's what I get for tryin to be nice to you. See if it ever happens again, you brat." She turned on her heel and stomped to the hallway. "I'm gonna tell Mom when she gets home tonight what's been goin on."

"She says you made her really mad. You're in for it now, Lacey." Ellie charged past her sister, wheeling about in front of her. "I told you not to make her angry, and now she won't let me play with her doll anymore! Thanks a lot, jerk head!" She pulled back her leg and kicked full force, connecting the toe of her scuffed Mary Jane with Lacey's shin. Hard. "I hate you!" she screamed, and ran down the stairs, leaving Lacey to limp alone in the dark.

"I am gonna kill that damn kid!" She growled to herself.

A note was tacked to the refrigerator by a watermelon shaped magnet. *Working a double. Have leftover casserole for dinner. Left extra money for ice cream. Love, Mom.* Lacey desperately needed to talk to their mom about Ellie's antics, but she didn't even see her in passing. As it turned out, Doralee got a second job to take up any extra time her regular job left available. When she announced her new schedule to Lacey, it was all she could do not to knock her mom's head against the wall.

"What about Ellie? Who's gonna take her to see Dr. Beakins?"

"She's fine, honey. I think she's been getting better. She probably doesn't even need to see the doctor anymore." Doralee pulled a gallon of milk from the refrigerator and poured a tall glass.

"Mom, she's got bruises all over her!"

"She's a very active young girl. Besides, all kids get bruises. It's completely normal."

"No, it's not," she insisted. "Besides, she keeps talking about this other girl…"

"You know she's always had that invisible friend. Most children do."

"I didn't have one. What if she's hallucinating?"

"God dammit, Lacey! She is FINE! What do you want from me? I've been workin my ass off to make sure you have what you need. Francine was nice enough to let us move in here so that you'd have a nice place to stay! And you're *still* not happy. You never are!" Doralee slammed the empty glass onto the counter so hard it should have shattered. "You have to be the most ungrateful girl I've ever known, and you have the nerve to sit there and complain about your baby sister! It's no wonder I stay away from here so much!"

That had ended the discussion about Ellie's medical treatment. Doralee had stormed out the kitchen and was gone again in minutes. Lacey was glued to her spot, completely caught off guard by her mother's reaction. They'd always had such a good relationship, so she never expected her mom to fly off the handle the way she did. She had been so stunned she couldn't even cry.

So Lacey wasn't surprised at another night alone with Ellie. It hadn't been so bad, the past week. Ellie was quiet, usually floating around the house, and hadn't said more than a couple words to Lacey since that evening on the third floor. There were a few times that Lacey thought she heard whispering, but when she would peak in on her sister, she would find her coloring quietly. Or sleeping.

This really started to bother her. Ellie never took naps. Not only was she sleeping more, but there were more bruises on her arms and legs. Soon, she started seeing cuts, too. But she couldn't get Ellie to talk to her, so all she could do was watch from a short distance and pray that she wouldn't have to call 911 for help.

A pan of leftover lasagna was left in the fridge, so Lacey preheated the oven and buttered some bread for toast. She decided that she would take Ellie to the mall for ice cream after dinner. A city bus stop was only a few blocks away, and some time out of that prison would probably do them both good. Perhaps she could get Ellie to talk to her over a chocolate chip sundae. She felt her spirits lifting at the idea. *It'll be okay*, she convinced herself. *I'll help her by myself and then...*

Her pep talk was interrupted by a blood curdling scream.

Only one scream. By the time she got to the second floor, she began to wonder if she hadn't imagined it. Making her rounds through all the rooms, she didn't find Ellie. Just as she feared, Ellie had to be on the third floor again. She almost didn't go, but she had to make sure Ellie wasn't causing trouble. So she steeled herself and headed up the dark stairwell.

A light shone from the same room Ellie had been playing in before, and Lacey marched directly down the hall to stand in the doorway. Her sister wasn't there. The attic door was open, though. *Please don't tell me she's in the attic,* Lacey thought. She approached the doorway cautiously. Pitch black greeted her, along with stifling silence.

"Ellie, are you up there?" Not so much as a tiny scuffle answered. "I'm not coming up there, Ellie. You need to come down here. NOW!"

Several minutes passed, and she heard nothing at all. No creaks, no groaning floorboards, no footsteps. If Ellie was somewhere in the dark attic, she was gonna stay there. Lacey had no intentions of looking for her. *She must've been hiding in one of the other rooms. Probably snuck back downstairs while I was in here looking.* She turned and made her way to the hall.

Met with more smothering black, she stretched her hands out, navigating down the dark corridor by touch. She could hear nothing but her own hesitant footsteps bearing on the aged wood floor. Ellie may have been a mean-spirited prankster, but she was too afraid of the dark to hide in the cavernous rooms on either side of the creepy passage. She was getting closer to the stairs so she quickened her pace, eager to descend to more comfortable realms.

It was the warm breath on the back of her neck that stopped her. Not only could she feel the deliberate exhale, but she could hear the soft whisper as it crawled across her skin. Unmistakable. She knew sooner or later Ellie would've shown herself, but Lacey was not at all amused. She tried to hide how shaken she was as she turned, her hands planted firmly on her hips.

"Very funny. I'm not......"

Her voice trailed off as she stared into the darkness. No retreating footsteps. No light at the far end of the hall. Her bravado died immediately. If Ellie was playing a trick on her, it was a damned good one. She turned and scrambled for the stairs, nearly tripping over her feet as she ran for escape. Her breath was rapid and labored.

She didn't stop until she reached the front door. Panting and shaking, she slumped against it, and waited for her heart to quit racing. A cold drink on the porch might settle her nerves. She glanced over her shoulder into the dim living room as she made her way towards the kitchen. And froze.

Ellie lay curled in a ball on the sofa. She was dead still, but the soft rasping indicated that she was sleeping. Lacey approached her slowly, steeling herself for the inevitable 'Boo!' she knew Ellie was saving for her, but as she drew close, Ellie didn't budge. Her eyes didn't even twitch. Her chest was rising and falling deeply; otherwise, she didn't move a muscle.

Lacey coughed, not on purpose, but it was enough to rouse Ellie. Her eyes opened slowly, and she squinted as she focused on her sister. Her response to the disruption was immediate hostility.

"What?"

"Were you just upstairs, Ellie?"

"No. I fell asleep."

"Right. Nice try, but I know you were up there."

"I was asleep. Quit buggin me."

"Buggin you? I was tryin to get dinner cooked when you started screaming. I don't have time for your games, Ellie."

She blinked a few times, confusion clearly visible in her eyes. She shook her head slowly, and glowered at Lacey. "Go make dinner, then. Leave me alone."

"Brat!" Back in the kitchen, Lacey finished the bread and casserole, and poured two glasses of iced tea. She was portioning the lasagna between two plates, focusing on menial tasks to take her mind off her edginess, convincing herself that she had imagined the incident upstairs. Then the thought hit her.

She felt the breath on her neck. Ellie was only as tall as her chest.

Either she'd had to jump, or stand on something to reach Lacey's neck. Whatever she did, there would have been a lot of noise. Not to mention, Lacey would have caught her in the act. Ellie wouldn't have made it down one flight of wooden stairs so quietly, never mind two flights. It wasn't just the breath that unnerved her, it was also the strong feeling that someone had been standing so close behind, they could have hugged her.

Ellie might've been telling the truth.

Lacey nearly dropped the glass in her hand. For the first time, she was actually afraid they were alone in the house. She knew their mom wouldn't be back anytime soon, and she had no idea where their aunt was, or when she'd be home. Usually Aunt Francine left before they woke in the mornings and arrived back home after they'd gone to bed.

Even Ellie's company would be preferable to being alone. Lacey placed their plates and glasses on a TV tray and joined her sister in the living room. She found the remote and turned on the television, surfing through the channels until she found a silly family sitcom to distract them both. They ate in silence.

Finally, Lacey cleared her throat, and painted a falsely cheerful smile on her face. "Wanna go for ice cream? Mom left us some money. It'd be nice to go out for a while." Ellie look unenthused by the suggestion. "Hey, I'll get you a pretzel, too. With mustard. It'll be fun."

"I'm tired," Ellie moaned. "I'm gonna go to bed now."

With that she pushed back her tray, leaving half her food untouched, and trudged to the stairway. Right before she went up she paused, looking over her shoulder at Lacey. There was something wrong, something peculiar. Her face. Barely discernable but still, Lacey had an overwhelming feeling that beneath her surface, something in Ellie wasn't merely a troublesome child. Not anymore.

The evening passed slowly without as much as a peep from Ellie. Lacey looked in on her many times, idly hoping to find her at play, but she remained in a deep sleep. Eventually, Lacey also decided to turn in for the night. Dinner dishes scrubbed clean and living room tidied, she climbed the stairs wearily, listening for phantom giggles or distant bumps. In her room were three table lamps and she left one on as she pulled her blankets to her chin and slipped into sleep.

Black waves carried her easily, a rolling tide floating her about in a dark oblivion. Faint distant shadows hovered on the edges of her vision, but she couldn't identify them. She could hear water breaking upon the shore as if she was approaching a beach, but the depths beneath her seemed endless. The calm was heaven. She dared not move lest she disturb the waters and plummet back to reality. She focused on her breathing, the sound of her pulse throbbing in her ears. Concentrated on the waves lightly cascading on black sand.

At first the whisper was faint, blending with the noises outside her. Perhaps it was in her head, or maybe it was swirling in stagnant pools above her head. She focused on the coming chant. No. It was actually beneath her, the hushed syllables. They grew in volume so slowly it seemed natural that suddenly the voice whispered directly in her ear.

"I'm here."

Lacey bolted upright. She was disoriented and trembling, struggling to recognize her surroundings. At first she thought she was still floating, but the firm mattress beneath her extinguished that hope. Pitch black still enveloped her, and it took only a moment to realize why it bothered her so much. The bedside lamp should have been lit.

The clock beside her lamp was dead as well. *Maybe the*

power's out, she reasoned, pulling her feet over the edge of the bed. She sat still, listening for any noise indicating her mom or Aunt Francine was awake. Dead silence. No evidence of anyone in her room. The voice in her dream had been simply that - in her dream. She stood, wavered a bit, and padded to the doorway.

"I'm here."

Her eyes popped open and she inhaled sharply. She clutched her sheets tightly. Where was she? It didn't feel like a dream, but wasn't she already awake? She pushed herself up on one elbow and glanced at her nightstand. The alarm clock read 3:27. She fumbled for the knob on her lamp, but it didn't relight. With just the red glow of her clock illuminating her room, she slowly
slipped from the warmth of her bed and shuffled quietly towards her door.

"I'm here."

I must still be dreaming. The voice wasn't a whisper; it resonated from somewhere very close by. A low rumble followed, not exactly a growl, but not exactly a laugh either. She glanced around her, straining her eyes to peer into the dark corners of the room. Sweeping the entirety of her bedroom, she came back to the door.

At first she thought the red glow was a reflection from her alarm clock, but it was too far away, tucked close to the floor by her doorway. She squatted down on her knees and leaned in closely, perplexed by the trick of light.

Two eyes met her's. Two eyes, a blank face, and the glint off the blade of a very long, very sharp knife. The blank face spread into a big grin. Then the black took over again.

Ellie wasn't touching her breakfast. The cereal floated in its milky pond until it turned to a gelatinous mush. Her appetite had steadily declined, despite Lacey's efforts to whip up the appetizing dishes that Ellie favored. She took two tiny sips of her orange juice and looked a Lacey with bloodshot eyes. Looked as if she hadn't slept in weeks, but actually, she was sleeping the better part of each day.

Lacey attempted once again to reason with her mother about Ellie, but when she mentioned Ellie's excessive sleep patterns, Doralee snapped. Lacey should've been happy Ellie was sleeping so much, if she was the bad child Lacey described. Once again, Lacey was accused of ingratitude and selfishness. The subject was unceremoniously dropped.

Meanwhile, Ellie had dark bags under her eyes. Lacey spotted more bruises and bite marks on her arms and legs, but every time she asked about them, Ellie clammed up. She wasn't playing with her toys so much, either. Sometimes when Lacey would check on her, she'd find her sitting in silence, staring into space. Even for the average, well-behaved child, that was extremely uncommon.

Fall heralded the start of a new school year, and the girls would be attending new schools. Lacey was looking forward to her junior year, but she was apprehensive of being in a different high school than all her friends. Ellie, on the other hand, was completely unaffected by the change, mostly because she didn't have friends. Lacey secretly hoped that the new schedule would snap Ellie back into her formerly precocious self. She was starting to miss the unreasonable temper tantrums and the childish name calling. Anything was better than watching her baby sister waste away.

School did seem to fire Ellie up, but not the way Lacey hoped. A week after classes started, Ellie's teacher pulled Lacey aside when she came to walk her sister home. Lacey could only imagine what the teacher was about to tell her, but she would've been wrong.

"Ms. Patrick, I need you to give your mother this letter." Mrs. Cheeks leaned in and discreetly slipped Lacey an envelope. "She needs to call me so we can set up a conference."

"Conference? For what?" Lacey was worried that Mrs. Cheeks noticed the marks on Ellie's body. The school probably suspected them of child abuse.

"Today Ellie assaulted one of her classmates. She spent most of the day in the guidance office. We did try to contact your mother, but she never returned our calls."

"She's been working a lot lately," Lacey mumbled, frowning at the envelope in her hand. "Uh, what did she do?"

"Just have your mother call us, dear. It's extremely important." Mrs. Cheeks glanced fleetingly at Ellie with a look that Lacey could swear was fear, and scampered away like a frightened rabbit, exiting the classroom without saying goodbye to either of the girls. Ellie was unaffected by her teacher's abrupt departure.

"Geesh, Ellie, what the hell happened? You just started fourth grade and they're already complaining about you. You're not gonna make it through the first month like this."

"I don't care. They're all stupid, anyway. I hate them." Ellie shrugged and pulled her backpack straps over her shoulders. Her expression registered no emotion. Lacey was immediately irritated.

She led Ellie out the doors and down the sidewalk. "You know, it's not nice to call them stupid. You're not exactly a pistol, yourself."

"Shut the hell up, you jackass. I didn't ask for your opinion."

Ellie stormed away, leaving Lacey open mouthed and at a loss for words. She composed herself and started after Ellie, and then remembered the envelope in her hand. Ellie knew how to get home by herself, so Lacey decided to follow at a distance. She tore open the envelope and skimmed the letter.

Dear Mrs. Patrick,

An immediate meeting is requested with you in regards to the inappropriate behavior of your daughter, Eleanor Patrick. If her behavior is not curtailed promptly, she will be facing a possible expulsion from this school. A school psychologist, as well as a city appointed social worker will also be in attendance.

Lacey turned around and headed back to the school. Her mother was going to avoid the school just as she avoided her daughters, so Lacey was determined to get an explanation from Mrs. Cheeks about the mystery meeting. She found Mrs. Cheeks seated at her desk, thumbing through class papers. She didn't see her standing in the doorway until Lacey cleared her throat.

"Ms. Patrick? I thought you had left." She shuffled papers nervously, avoiding Lacey's eyes.

"I need to know what happened today."

"I'll discuss it with your mother, dear."

"Look, Mrs. Cheeks, my mother is sick. Deathly sick. So, I..." She fumbled for an excuse. "I need to tell my aunt what's going on. Cause she's too busy to come to the school for a meeting. So she asks me to help her. With Ellie." She hoped she was a believable liar.

"You said a few minutes ago that your mother was working a lot," the teacher pointed out. "Ellie never mentioned her mother's illness."

"We didn't want anyone to know."

"And how long has she been sick?"

"Oh... years. She's got a rare form of cancer. So rare it doesn't even have a name yet." She added quickly, "They're thinking of naming it after her."

"Huh. I see." Mrs. Cheeks didn't look like she believed Lacey's story, but after studying her for a minute, she motioned to a chair and said, "Have a seat, Lacey."

Lacey sat in a small red chair, and watched as Mrs. Cheeks closed the door. After she situated herself behind the desk once again, she regarded Lacey once more, as if trying to decide how much she was going to tell her.

"After lunch on Tuesdays, the class goes to the library. They spend about twenty minutes of free time, either reading or working on their assignments. The kids really enjoy library time." She paused, waiting for Lacey's response. Lacey simply nodded and waited for her to continue.

"Today, as a few of the girls were browsing through the stacks, Ellie and another child began to argue. I'm still not clear how the argument started, because by the time we were aware of the altercation, they'd already been pulled apart. From what the other children told me," she leaned in close and her voice dropped to a near whisper, "Ellie struck the other girl four times in the head with a large book, and then bit her."

"She bit her? Lots of kids bite. You expel children for biting each other?"

"Of course not. Normally. But Ellie left a rather large cut on the young lady's head, and then she... she bit a *chunk* out of her cheek."

Lacey sat immobilized. The visual image painted was nothing short of an actual monster. Mrs. Cheeks continued, "She's going to need at least a dozen stitches. The parents will most likely press charges. And your mother will be held accountable for your sister's behavior." She pushed her glasses back and straightened her shoulders. "I really am sorry to hear about your mother's condition, Ms. Patrick. In such extreme situations, children are often sent to homes for juvenile delinquents. And there's also foster care. The social worker plans to discuss that at the meeting."

"I can't tell my mother about this, Mrs. Cheeks. It'll do her in. Can't I just talk to Ellie? Get her to promise to behave?"

"Honestly, Lacey, I wish it were that simple. But quite frankly, I don't think Ellie can be trusted. She doesn't act like her peers. She doesn't act like a child at all. She acts like a... Well." She stood up quickly, and gestured for Lacey to follow her out.

"I'll tell her. And I will talk to Ellie. Tonight. I'm sure she's real sorry." Lacey smiled and tried to make herself believe what she was saying, but the knot in her stomach said otherwise.

She took the long way home, replaying the conversation in her head. Stomach queasy, she looked for some rationale to Ellie's bizarre actions. The fear she saw in her teacher's eyes mirrored the growing fears that Lacey was experiencing at home. Without the intervention of her mother, she knew she was powerless to control Ellie. What was she going to do?

The passing buildings escaped her notice as she trudged the streets of downtown, sidewalks strewn with garbage and vagrants. She paid no heed to the people sidling past her, thoughts racing like a freight train through her head. Children chased each other in circles around the stoops of a few town homes, dogs yipping at their heels. Sounds of a reality she had never known. A safer reality.

"Aren't you too warm in that coat?"

Lacey stopped and looked around. Sitting on the sidewalk against a vandalized brick wall, an old lady was watching her. Her hair was a dirty brown streaked with grey, and her clothes were as grimy as her skin. Lacey took a step in her direction warily, confused by her absurd remark. It was still at least seventy five degrees outside, and Lacey was wearing short sleeves.

"I'm not wearing a coat," she pointed out.

"You wear a coat. I wear a coat. Everybody wears a coat. Outside." The derelict laughed and shook her head. Her hands trembled as they smoothed over her ragged skirt. "Everyone in a coat. That's always the way. Problem is there's not enough coats."

"In this town?"

"No! Here. All around us. In this," she motioned around herself, "Space."

"You could always buy a new one."

"No!" Psycho lady sputtered, "You can't buy coats."

"Right," Lacey said, backing away from the lunatic. "I think I'd better get going."

"Watch your coat, now. Don't let it get stolen!"

The cackles followed her down the sidewalk as she quickened her pace. *Crazy old bat*, she thought to herself. Summer still rallied for attention, as it would for several more weeks. Who cared about coats when she was still wearing shorts to school? "They should round up the bums and drive them out of town," Lacey grumbled softly.

The nut job was quickly forgotten. Lacey had far more serious things to worry about. Without her mother's help, she would be fail to improve Ellie's habits. It was time to go around her mother and look for outside assistance. She would find Dr. Beakins' number and ask for an emergency appointment. Certainly he would agree there was a need for urgent treatment.

The house was silent when she arrived, but Ellie's book bag was dumped on the kitchen counter, so she knew she'd made it home okay. She located an out of date phone book buried under a pile of papers in the breezeway. Pen in hand, she searched through hundreds of doctors' listings, soon spotting Dr. Beakins listed under pediatricians. Peeking into the living room to make sure Ellie wasn't within earshot, she dialed the number and waited on hold for a receptionist.

"Dr. Beakins' office, how may I help you?"

"I need to make an appointment for my sister, please."

"Are you her legal guardian?"

"Well, no. But I live with her." She knew already what they would say.

"If you're not her legal guardian, then you need a power of attorney before you can make doctor's appointments."

"How do I get one?" She knew she was beginning to sound desperate.

"Your mother would need to file one and have it notarized. Otherwise, there's nothing we can do for you."

Lacey's voice broke. "Please? This is a real emergency."

"I'm sorry, dear. My hands are tied. If it's an emergency you can call 911." The receptionist sounded more impatient than sorry.

Lacey placed the receiver on its cradle and heavily took a seat at the kitchen table. The ordeal was taking its toll on her, as her emotions swung from worry to anger from one week to the next. No matter what she did, Ellie would continue to deteriorate, and as she did, she would take Lacey down with her. Forget going out with friends, forget dating. Forget her prom. She was tied down by the creature her sister had become and there was no light ahead. No ray of light.

Resentment flooded her like a breeched levy. Ellie was NOT gonna destroy her! She was tired of being victimized by her sister's animosity. She didn't care what her mother had to say. If Ellie didn't respond to reason, then she would respond to an old fashioned ass beating. Lacey stood so fast she knocked over the chair, and bound up the steps two at a time. Her anger was building momentum as she crashed into Ellie's bedroom.

Empty. *Not this again!* "Ellie! Where the hell are you?" She screamed. "We are going to talk. NOW!" She was not at all surprised when Ellie didn't answer.

She bolted up the stairs to the third floor. This time she would not be intimidated. She was psyching herself up for the confrontation, ready to knock her sister into oblivion. Fueled by fury, it didn't take five seconds to reach the room as she ran down the black hallway. The door stood open, the lamp glowed a sickly light.

Ellie wasn't inside.

Lacey was growing vexed of Ellie's hide and seek. She turned to leave, when the voice stopped her. It was a vague echo, resonating from somewhere in the room. No, not in the room. Above the room. In the attic. "Ellie, get your ass down here and talk to me!" No footsteps, no reply. Nothing. "The cops are here and they're gonna arrest you!" It was a lie and she doubted it would work. She was right.

The murmuring continued, unresponsive to her commands. She raced downstairs, and foraged through the kitchen pantry, searching for an old lantern she'd seen there before. After a couple smacks against her palm, the flashlight threw a weak beam of light on the wall. She flew back up the stairs and didn't stop until she was at the attic entrance. Mustering every ounce of courage she had, she crept quietly as possible up the dark stairs.

Cobwebs swayed above her, dancing in smothering drafts of hot air. She could hear the voice louder now, but still couldn't understand the words. More disembodied laughter. The murmurs morphed into a muffled chant that circled faster above her. Each step led her up into an oven of thick air.

The voice died as Lacey announced her presence. "Ellie, this shit has got to stop!"

The attic wasn't dark, as she supposed. A single light bulb jutted from a wall fixture, illuminating the dusty confines of the small room. Rafters sharply angled either side; puffy pink insulation crammed into crevices above her head and peeked through the makeshift floor boards. Boxes and crates were stacked against the walls, but there was furniture as well. An antique mahogany wardrobe with mirrored doors stood on the far side of the room. An iron bed frame was propped against some boxes, and an aged mattress commandeered most of the floor space. There were a few trunks with large foreboding hasps lying about, and one of them was opened.

Lacey was spellbound, so much so that she didn't notice Ellie wasn't in the attic. She navigated her way to the wardrobe, and rummaged through dresses hung on ratty hangers. The dresses were about as old as the dresses her mother had saved from her youth. The smell of mothballs and mildew clung to the various fabrics, and she pulled one out to get a better look. Once a yellow dress, it had a flared skirt, and was decorated with a white collar, pearl buttons down the bodice, and a cracked patent leather belt. She tossed the dress on the mattress and headed for the trunk.

Inside was a jumble of personal effects; A tangle of chunky beads, three hats flattened by six hardcover books, an empty silver trinket box that had tarnished. She also found handkerchiefs and socks, a beaded clutch, and a dozen or so 45rpm records, most cracked and scratched beyond repair. And at the bottom of the trunk rested a large photo album.

She dug out the album from under the chaos and flopped down on the mattress, oblivious to the dust balls that danced around her. The thick green cover crackled as she carefully opened to the first page. Deeply faded pages the color of old newsprint displayed numerous old photos in different shapes and sizes. Some were black and white, some were faded colors, and all were held in place by tiny black corners. There were vacation shots, Christmas pictures. *Their family pictures*, Lacey thought. She recognized her mom and Aunt Francine at different ages in many of the photographs. Scattered throughout were the faces of cousins, aunts, uncles, some who she never met.

Flipping through the pages, she found a large picture glued to a page by itself. Ink scrawled beneath the image labeled the three young teenage girls smiling prettily at the photographer. The flowing cursive was barely legible, but she finally deciphered the scrawl.

Doralee, Nancy, and Francine, spring, 1973.'

She had no idea who Nancy was. The young woman was blonde, attractive, and dressed in a wrap around shirt and denim jeans. Her hair grazed her shoulders, and her eyes were so large Lacey could clearly see they were vibrantly blue. She looked a lot like Ellie.

She browsed through more of the album, but there weren't very many pictures of Nancy. There were, however, quite a few empty spaces left by photos that had been removed. She frowned, turning pages almost frantically, searching for more pictures of the mystery girl. She found one more, somewhere close to the back of the book. Legs folded together primly, her polite smile and shining eyes the epitome of social grace, Nancy was uncommonly pristine. Lacey was taken aback by how proper she appeared, especially considering how much she resembled Ellie. There was another scraggly caption written beneath.

Nancy Eleanora Thomassy, 13 years old.

She had been only four years older than Ellie in the picture, and yet she seemed much older. More mature. Impeccably groomed and meticulously stylish. She wore a white hat, white gloves, white shoes. And a yellow dress with pearl buttons down the bodice.

She looked around at Nancy's things. Why would her belongings be shoved away in Aunt Francine's attic? There were no other pictures of Nancy. No reason why the young woman disappeared completely from her family's lives. She rummaged again through the trunk but came up empty handed. The other trunks were locked tight and she couldn't pick them open. She must've walked over the folded piece of newsprint a dozen times before she noticed it beneath her shoe.

It turned out to be two pieces of newspaper clippings folded together. One was an obituary, half the ink rubbed off and the tiny picture smeared beyond recognition. The other was an article, dated April 18, 1974. The headline ominously answered the questions whirling in her mind.

Tragic Fire Claims the Life of a Local Area Teen

  Nancy Thomassy, second daughter to Harold and Bernadette Thomassy, perished in a house fire that destroyed half of the Phelps Park residence. Mr. and Mrs. Thomassy were not home at the time of the fire, but their two other daughters, Francine and Doralee Thomassy, escaped without injury. Nancy was rushed to the Sinclair Medical Center, where she was declared dead upon arrival. Investigators are still determining the cause of the fire.

  Still, she couldn't rationalize the secrecy. There were pictures of countless family members all over the house, but not even as much as one snapshot of Nancy anywhere. The sisters had done their best to wipe Nancy's existence from everyone's memory, so why was Ellie given her name?

  Lacey wouldn't waste her breath pressing her mother for an explanation. But there was someone else who knew the truth, and while Lacey never had many real conversations with her, she knew how to get her to talk. Carefully, she pried the portrait from the worn page of the book and returned the album to its resting place. Tucking the dress back into the wardrobe and making certain that all was where she'd found it, she exited the attic.

  Francine was nearly as much a workaholic as Doralee, and although Lacey attempted to wait up, she dozed off before her aunt arrived home. Fortunately, her alarm clock buzzed her awake bright and early, and she tiptoed downstairs to lie in wait for her unsuspecting victim.

  Unbeknownst to her, Lacey was sitting at the kitchen table when Francine came in for her morning coffee. She froze when she saw her niece waiting with two mugs of steaming java. "Oh. Hello, Lacey. You're up earlier than I'd expected."

  "I really need to talk to you, Francie. I think it might be

important."

"Don't you think it would be best to speak with your mother, then?"

Lacey huffed. "She doesn't exactly talk to me anymore. There's no one else to talk to."

"Are you pregnant?"

"What? No! Why would you think I..." She sighed, took a small sip of her coffee, and lowered her voice. "It's about Nancy."

"Who?" Francine paled considerably. The expression on her face was pure guilt. Lacey was certain she'd find her answers. "I don't know a Nancy."

"Then who is the girl in this picture?" Lacey pulled the portrait of Nancy from her lap and placed it between them on the Formica table. Francine opened her mouth to speak, most likely a refusal, but Lacey interrupted. "Before you deny it, I know Ellie was named after her."

They regarded each other silently for what felt like an eternity. "Oh, fine," Francine muttered. "I told her you would find out about it sooner or later, but she insisted we shouldn't ever tell you."

"Tell me what? About the fire that killed your sister?"

"If you know about it, then why ask me?"

"I was in the attic. I saw the news article. I don't know what the big deal is. Accidents happen, I mean, houses catch fire all the time. A lot of times, its bad wiring. Why hide our aunt from us?"

Francine took a deep breath. "It wasn't an accident. Nancy was murdered. She was doused with lighter fluid and set on fire. That's why only the garage was destroyed."

Lacey couldn't speak. It felt as if someone had dumped ice over her head. She struggled to fathom what her aunt was telling her, but she hadn't expected such a confessional. Her voice was a cracked whisper. "But... why? Who killed her, Francie?" She scrambled for reasoning. "It was a burglary gone wrong, wasn't it?" Surely that was all.

Francine cleared her throat, her hands trembling as she sipped her coffee. "Your mother did it," Francine stopped her before she could respond. "Please, hear me out first." She got up from the table, poured herself another cup of coffee, and seated herself across from Lacey once more.

"We were afraid of Nancy. Actually, we were terrified of her. Even though she was several years younger than me, she was... different. See, when Nancy was about seven, she told your mother and me that she had this special 'gift'. She claimed she could leave her body and go places without anyone knowing about it."

Lacey stared at her aunt like she had lost her mind. Francine continued.

"We did notice there were times when Nancy would zone out. Like she was catatonic. At first, it was only for minutes at a time, but eventually, she would blank out for hours. When she'd snap out of it, she'd tell us these outlandish stories of things she had done, many of them very harmful to other people. Yes, we were very terrified. Especially your mother. We'd become convinced she was telling us the truth. Doralee swore that Nancy was some sort of demon. You remember your grandparents, right? How religious they were? We went to church four times every week. We didn't want our parents to know what their daughter was, it would have killed them. So Doralee decided that we'd take care of it ourselves."

Lacey swallowed hard. "What... what did you do?"

"Mom and Dad were out for the evening. Some charity event; I don't really recall now. I asked Nancy if she could find the hammer in the garage for me, and your mom was hiding inside behind the door. When Nancy passed by, Doralee struck her in the head with a baseball bat. It didn't kill her, but we hadn't expected it would. We'd already made other plans, anyway. Your mom grabbed a can of lighter fluid and poured it all over Nancy, and struck a match. We hoped she would stay unconscious, but she came to when the flames covered her legs. We'd run out of there and locked her in, so she couldn't get to the water." Francine stared numbly at the wall behind Lacey. "Didn't expect her to scream so much."

Shaking herself visibly, she refocused on Lacey. "We called the fire department once Nancy's screams stopped. We were kind of surprised they stopped so quickly, but we were relieved. We weren't trying to burn the house down, and we knew a fire in the garage would be easily containable. And Mom and Dad would never have to know the truth. We never discussed it again, not with anybody. Told the investigators there was an open bottle of lighter fluid on a shelf, and Nancy had been using a match to see. It was a freak accident. No one asked any more questions."

Lacey recalled the breath on her neck. The strange detached laughter floating in the halls. Perhaps Nancy was haunting the house? That would explain so much. Perhaps she was a poltergeist and was beating on Ellie whenever she felt like it. "Do you think she's gone, Francie?"

"Of course, she is! That's an absurd question! She's been dead and buried for 33 years now." She rose, took her mug to the sink. "You kids watch too many horror movies." Sitting down heavily in her chair, she picked up the photograph and stared at it for the longest time, eyes watering. "She was beautiful, though."

Lacey was about to go back to her bedroom. She had only a half hour to get dressed for school and Ellie wasn't awake yet. She paused, turned to gaze at Francine's slumped back. One more question.

"Why did you decide to tell me all this?"

"I need a clear conscious. I've been hiding this so long I think it's eating me alive. I don't want this burden anymore."

Francine was still frozen in place when the girls left for school. Ellie gazed quizzically at her aunt, and stopped before Lacey could pull her out the door. "Aren't you going to work, Francie?"

"I'm not feeling so good today, dear. Think I'll make a doctor's appointment." She didn't look at either of the girls. They left her alone with her guilty conscious.

Lacey tried hard to focus on her lessons, but she was distracted by Francine's story. That her mother had spent the past three decades hiding such an unspeakable crime almost made her pity the woman. All the same, her bitterness towards the woman who'd been neglecting them was palpable. She stewed silently most of the morning, tuning out her teachers' voices completely. Until a loudspeaker announcement slapped her into awareness.

"Ms. White, would you please send Lacey Patrick to the office?" Her classmates erupted in the obligatory "Oooo!" as she gathered her books and left the room. The hard granite floors echoed her footsteps like a countdown to her doom, but she hadn't done anything that would warrant a visit to the principle.

"You have a phone call, Lacey," the secretary informed her, offering her the receiver.

She brought it to her ear, and hesitantly said, "Hello?"

"Lacey, this is Mrs. Cheeks, Ellie's teacher."

"Yes?"

"It seems Ellie has disappeared. We haven't seen her since lunch. Do you know where she could be?" The tone of her voice was accusatory, as if she believed the sisters were conspiring against her.

"I dropped her off at school this morning and I haven't seen her since. I've been in classes all day. All my teachers will tell you that," she was sure she sounded defensive.

"Well, I tried contacting your mother, but once again, she hasn't returned my call. Sick or not, I'm tempted to call child welfare and have this investigated."

"That won't be necessary, Mrs. Cheeks, I promise. Ellie was

probably sick and went home. She hasn't been herself lately."

"Her behavior is inexcusable, Ms. Patrick. Just so you're aware, she will probably be suspended for leaving school property in the middle of the day without permission or parental supervision."

"Yes. Thank you, Mrs. Cheeks," she mumbled, placing the receiver in the secretary's waiting hand. "I need to leave. I need to find my sister." There were three women behind the front counter, and they all stared at her like she'd lost her mind.

A woman with tightly curled hair and a pinched expression stepped forward. "That would be a matter for your parents to handle. You need to return to class now, young lady."

Lacey had about enough. She'd been trying her best to keep everything together, but she was only 16, after all. She glared at the staff and fought the urge to tell them each to go to hell. Instead, she steadied her voice, and said very evenly, "I am leaving now. I don't care what you say. Go ahead and suspend me." She turned on her heel and marched out, turning towards the front entrance rather than back to her class.

She practically ran down the street. Without any idea where Ellie had headed, the only place she knew to check was home. Didn't make sense for Ellie to go anywhere else. There was a public park on the way, and she stopped momentarily to look. Maybe Ellie was playing at the playground. No signs of any children anywhere. She made her way back to the street without noticing the woman on a bench.

"Your coat needs mending."

She stopped, approached the woman angrily. It was a bad time for the bum's psychotic harassment. "Lady, what the *hell* are you talking about? Its seventy degrees outside! You need to lay off the bottle before you piss off the wrong person!"

Old Crazy stood up, hobbled towards her. She reeked of alcohol and urine and body odor, but as she drew near, Lacey could see that her eyes were sharp, not bloodshot. And while her face was streaked with dirt, it appeared the grime floated outside her skin. Like she was wearing a transparent costume. Lacey took a step back from her advance.

"Don't be such a fool. You're hearing is as ill-suited as your coat."

Lacey grunted and backed away. "I got better things to worry about than you. Seriously, you should go to a shelter, or something. Not everyone is as nice as me."

As she ran away, the woman shouted at her back. "You best take heed! Some would kill to have a coat like yours!"

Aunt Francine's car was still in the driveway. Lacey wondered that the school hadn't called the house about Ellie. She busted in the door, fully expecting to see Ellie in front of the television. She was met with dead quiet, and no signs of her sister.

"Ellie?" When there was no reply, "Aunt Francie?" Francine's room was empty. She peeked into the cluttered garage, hoping to find her aunt busy at some task, but the lights were off and there was no movement in the darkness. Kitchen, pantry, laundry room, living room. Still no signs of either her aunt or sister.

Creeping up the stairs, back to the wall, Lacey tried to remain unobtrusive, largely because she didn't relish the notion of any surprise encounters. Despite caution, she was certain her heart was pounding so loudly it echoed through the stairway. The ticking of a wall clock reverberated from the living room a signal that she best keep her guard up. She made it to the second floor uneventfully, and slipped quickly to Ellie's bedroom. What a waste of time.

She knew Ellie wasn't in her room. Instinctively, she hadn't expected to see her sister quietly completing homework or playing with her dolls. Just as she convinced herself that a trip to the third floor was necessary, a noise from outside Ellie's window startled her. Verging upon the window, she opened the sash to look out over Francine's backyard. The ground was already covered in dried leaves.

Throwing herself down the stairs, she ran for the back door. Of course! Francine was in the yard with the rake. She flung open the screen door and bolted around the corner of the house. And stopped cold.

One leg was completely bent underneath her body, the other twisted nearly completely backwards. The torso was arched upwards, or so it seemed. As she drew near to her aunt's body, she realized quickly that her torso wasn't arched. Something was protruding through her chest, and had pushed her denim shirt forward. The front of her shirt was soaked in a nearly black wetness. Her left arm was torn at the cuff and trapped under her head. And her head... oh god! Her head was split open, the ground underneath soaked deep red, and speckled with bits of slimy gray matter.

Lacey stumbled backwards, landing hard on her ass as she shoved her fist in her mouth, fighting to suppress a scream. Her stomach heaved violently, and she leaned forward between her spread legs, vomiting everything in her stomach. She didn't try to move; instead she propped her head weakly in her hands and sobbed mere feet from the gore that used to be Francie.

Eventually, she pulled her head up, but averted her eyes away, fearful she would be sick once more. She focused on the faded shingles of the house, the tired olive green shutters banking each window. Her gaze traveled up the side of the house, noting how the house seemed to hover over her, her eyes coming to rest on the third floor open window. A sheer curtain from within billowed lightly into the breeze.

Vision locked on the yawning darkness, Lacey pulled herself to her feet and sidestepped her way back around the corner of the house. The screen door shrieked as she threw it open, stepped into the cool gray and bolted the door behind her. Tripping over a piece of ripped linoleum, she staggered to the telephone and prepared to dial 911.

A large crash shattered the stillness from somewhere above Lacey's head. She couldn't imagine Ellie making such a loud ruckus, and she refused to fathom that Ellie could've pushed their aunt from the window. After all, the worst of Ellie's violence had always been turned on herself. Someone else was in the house. Lacey tiptoed to the garage and found a small hatchet propped against the wall. Brandishing her weapon in front of her, she prepared herself with the confrontation she knew would result when she located the intruder.

The third floor was eerily peaceful. Lacey took the time to briefly peer into each room, vague traces of sunlight barely illuminating their confines. Surprisingly, they all appeared to be bedrooms, but for whom Lacey didn't know. Didn't seem to matter so much at the moment. She didn't give second thought to the fact that most of the beds looked slept in, comforters rumpled, pillows indented. She descended upon the room with the opened window, and slowly stepped inside, holding the hatchet out farther in front.

No one there. Not under the bed, not inside the musty old closet. The comforter had been pulled partially from the bed, pointing toward the window. Francine must have grabbed onto it before she fell. As she swept the walls a final time, she spotted something peculiar. She stepped closer for a better look. Now she knew what was embedded in Francine's back.

The walls were discolored from neglect, and the pictures left outlines where they'd been displayed. A few frames had been knocked off their hooks and left bright squares about the walls. Apparently, there were more than just pictures decorating the room. One of the shapes was the distinct outline of a short handled dagger. Lacey began to feel nauseous again. Francine wasn't merely pushed from the window.

Backing from the room slowly, Lacey grasped the doorknob and pulled the door closed with her, nervously straining her eyes to peer into the gloomy corridor. Not a soul to be found. And then the ambiguous rhythm of a whispered chant circled her. The words were indiscernible, but she wasn't concerned with their meaning. She followed their trail to the attic door.

As she followed the incantation up the rickety dark stairs, the words became more audible. *"Inside out and outside in...."* The same words, over and over, faster and faster.

She didn't understand their meaning, but as soon as she emerged into the suffocating alcove, the chanting stopped. Her eyes adjusted slowly to the dimly lit room as she surveyed the neglected items strewn about, all exactly as she had left them. Well, except for Ellie's doll, the one that belonged to '*her*'.

Her gaze lighted on the ragged doll, breath caught in her throat. Last she'd seen of the doll, it was laid across Ellie's pillows. Lacey approached the abandoned doll, despair gnawing at her gut. Ellie was somewhere in the house. Which meant that either Ellie was hurt, possibly dead, or she was the culprit. Lacey wasn't sure what scared her the most.

Bending to pick up the doll, something caught Lacey's attention from the corner of her eye. To her far right, she saw smoke. Just a wispy tendril that curved a few times, and then dissipated. After a moment, it reappeared. Fearing the small beginnings of a fire, she tossed her hatchet on the mattress and converged upon the location, finding nothing unusual upon her inspection. She was so distracted she didn't hear the arriving footsteps behind her.

"What are you doing?" Ellie was nonchalant, completely unfazed by her sister's intrusion. She slid past Lacey and glanced at the phantom smoke, and chuckled briefly. "Oh, that." She swiped it with a wave of her hand and flopped onto the mattress. "That's no big deal."

"What?" Lacey gaped open mouthed at her sister, and then sputtered, "There's something really wrong here, and you don't seem the least bit concerned about it." Her eyes narrowed suspiciously, and she hovered over the mattress. "You killed Aunt Francie, didn't you?"

Ellie's eyes blazed at her furiously, her mouth twisted in a maniacal grimace. Her voice was a grating taunt. "Don't be stupid. How could I do that? I'm just a kid. You say so all the time."

"Not the time to be a smart-ass, Ellie," Lacey threatened evenly. "Why don't you look in the back yard? Francine is dead."

"I know. I saw her already." She stood slowly, tossed her doll over her shoulder.

"I swear to god, Ellie, I'm gonna go call the police to report a murder, and when I do, I'm gonna tell them I think you did it." Lacey poked her finger into Ellie's chest, expecting to see some glimmer of fear in their blue depths.

But instead, Ellie stepped back, a strange calm expression sliding over her face as she studied her sister. "Really? You think you can?" Her voice was cold and hollow. Lacey glanced at Ellie's wrists and saw another bite mark, this one fresh. Blood still glistened where teeth had broken her skin. Her protective instincts kicked in, and she grasped Ellie's arm, horrified by her injury. Ellie pulled her arm away and stepped back.

"I don't understand what's going on with you, Ellie. Really, I don't think you killed Francine, but you act like you're possessed or something. I think maybe you need to go to the hospital."

"I don't need a fucking hospital. I need you to leave me alone," she spat.

"Please, Ellie. Let me go call the doctor. You're bleeding." Lacey pleaded.

Ellie looked at her wrist as if it was the first time she had noticed the mark. Her face drained of all color and she stared at Lacey with panicked eyes. "I didn't do it. Honest." No sooner than she uttered the words, an eerie smile crossed her face, and she raised her wounded wrist to her lips. Twisting her battered arm slightly, she bit into her flesh, sinking her teeth deep into her skin until crimson drops ran over her arm and rained around her feet.

"Ellie!" Lacey shrieked, lunging at her and prying her arm from her mouth. "Stop it! You've lost your mind! I'm calling 911..."

"Get your hands of me."

Ellie's voice was deep. A deliberate warning that should have fallen from someone else's lips. Lacey's skin covered in gooseflesh as she watched Ellie's head suddenly drop to her chest, like a puppet whose strings had been cut. Her mouth fell open, and Lacey saw the distinct tendrils of smoke dance from Ellie's mouth. The smoke curled and shimmered and shifted into the vague outline of a woman.

Lacey was rooted to her spot, staring in morbid fascination at the writhing figure that moved steadily closer. Vaporous appendages snaked forward, combing through Lacey's hair. It felt like cold needles prickling her scalp. They caressed her cheeks, lifted her chin, slid across her lips almost seductively. Suddenly, Lacey experienced what felt like a cinderblock ram into her chest, knocking her breath out of her as she tumbled backwards. She pulled herself to her feet, steadied by some nearby boxes, and searched for the apparition. Instead, she saw herself, wavering on her feet for a moment before she toppled onto the mattress.

As the shadow of herself, she could see Nancy more clearly, the cynical twist of her grin, the glinting menace in her steel blue eyes. Their breaths both smoked wispy tendrils in the freezing chill of what once was a stifling hot attic. Both drew their gazes to Lacey's prostrate body, and she knew without doubt what Nancy was planning. She dove for her body, slipping inside her skin like a warm glove. "Everyone in a coat....." She finally understood.

"Lacey? Are you there?" Ellie had regained conscious, peering anxiously into her sister's face. Her small hands tugged at Lacey's arms, and she was whimpering desperately, trying to pull Lacey to her feet. Nancy shivered forward, wrapped around a lock of Ellie's hair and plucked her from Lacey's hold.

Her voice was a serpentine hiss. "She took from me, so I take from her."

"No! Not Ellie, you bitch!" Lacey ran headlong into Nancy's shifting shape, and seized Ellie's arm. It was not unlike running into a wall of dry ice. She wrenched Ellie from her grasp and pulled her back with her. "We gotta get out of here!" She shouted. But Ellie didn't hear her.

She heard Ellie's scream just before her sister flew across the attic, bouncing off the boxes. Lacey met the glare of the girl looking out from Ellie's eyes. The vicious beast seethed pure hatred, her teeth bared and bloody from her assault on Ellie's arm. "Give her back!" Lacey warned.

"Or what? You're such a pathetic fool, Lacey," Nancy snarled back at her.

Lacey could see her sister cowering by the wardrobe, no more than a few feet from Nancy. She shouted to her sister, "Ellie, push her back! You can push her out!"

Ellie shimmered hesitantly, but briefly. She threw herself at her body with hands outstretched, her mist absorbing into her skin as an evil cry shook the attic. Lacey grabbed her sister's hand, trying to escape the brunt of Nancy's rage.

Nancy reeled like a cyclone, gathering momentum as she hovered overhead. She pulled back, took her aim, and shot straight at Lacey, barreling directly into her chest. She felt herself being pushed off her feet, felt the smack of the floor against her back. She'd been displaced again, but even as she gathered herself, she knew something was different. She watched confusion clouding her eyes, seized by alarm.

"Lacey? Wha... what happened?" Ellie looked down at hands that were much larger than her own. She turned circles, not comprehending that the misty swirl in front of her was Lacey's soul. Lacey saw her approach and screamed for Ellie's attention, but Ellie couldn't hear her above the deafening cry Nancy roared as she sprang forward and buried the hatchet in Ellie's back. Ellie cried out, blood seeping from the corners of her mouth in rivulets of crimson. Time suspended, and then Lacey watched her sister fall over, taking Lacey's torn body with her.

She stared. No tears. No screams. Her blood sputtered around the blade like a geyser, pouring over her shoulder blades, pooling around her head and chest. *It's just my body,* she told herself. *I'm okay. It's just my body.*

She gathered herself together much like carrying a bundle of frozen laundry. Levitating just above the floor, she searched for Ellie. She saw her standing before one of the wardrobe door mirrors, combing her fingers daintily through her hair and smoothing her skirt. Catching Lacey's gaze in the mirror, she slowly smiled. Wickedly. The ice blue of her stare chilled Lacey that much more.

"Where's Ellie?" Lacey whimpered. She searched the shadowed corners for smoky curls.

"She died in your body. She won't be back." Nancy replied in a sing-song voice.

"No."

"She didn't get out in time. Pity."

Lacey was stuck between worlds without a body. *Without a coat.* She watched helpless as Nancy scooped Ellie's doll off the floor, turned off the single light bulb, and left her in a dark limbo. The words drifted back to haunt her…

"Everyone in a coat. That's always the way. Problem is there's not enough coats."

The End

FOOD CHAINS
By John Miller

He rots.

Like so many of his kind, the potential to unleash his powers upon mortals, to destroy them utterly, to sap their life force through consumption of their blood, is his to wield like a blade in the hand of a berserker. Oh, yes! He possesses this power; it's in his blood. That's the secret: blood.

The cessation of rot is all about the blood. Consume blood and he won't rot. Not any more. All he has to do is climb out of his coffin, use his vampiric methods to obfuscate his form, sneak behind a hapless mortal, mesmerize them with hypnotic eyes...drink their blood.

There's a trick to it; it's not that easy. Not even when you've drunk a hundred mortals dry. Conscience remains for a vampire while, perhaps, the soul flees...downward? It doesn't matter where his soul resides—he cannot feel it. All that matters is the blood; it helps stop the rot.

He senses footfalls. Vibrations escalate, and sound finally reaches him and confirms the vibrations. Two mortals approach. One weighs over two-hundred pounds. This one has the gait of a man, the brash steps of bravado over the hidden face of death unknown. The other mortal weighs around one-hundred and fifty pounds, probably his lover. Yes, he can smell her now, her Chardonnay wafts in the wind and permeates even through the soil, and it fills his coffin. Is it a supernatural power that allows her scent to fill his underground home and mask the stink of rot? Does it matter?

Subtle noises... claws that scratch vibrate below...so far below. The sewers, full of rodents, wharf rats the size of small dogs.

He waits until the mortals above walk over his grave. When they're gone, his mind exits his body. He feels the smoothness of skull, gray membrane and thinly stretched flesh pass through his perceptions—he is outside his body now. His mind travels downward through the small tunnel, follows its path toward the stink of human feces and urine. His mind, disconnected from his physical body, falls out of the hole into a large sewer tunnel. Wharf rats, sewer rats, ordinary rats—they're all here.

"Come to me, my pets!" he mentally thinks in the form of imagined shout. His mental command assaults the rodents with his enhanced mental prowess. "Come to stop the rot!"

Five large wharf rats scurry up the sewer wall and push into the tunnel. He follows with his mind, and races them to his body. Adhemar beats them to his body, and he reintegrates within himself, feels his cold flesh animate. He holds the mesmerized rats close to his chest, a group hug. "Come to daddy!"

Twin incisors slide into rat flesh. He tastes wet fur, foulness, muscles twitch beneath his crimson lips. Adhemar does this to maintain his humanity, to safeguard his conscience from pain. He hadn't asked to become one of the undead, but he must exist in this state. He remembers Clarice.

"You think you maintain your humanity?" Clarice asked him a decade ago. "You think sucking on the shitty fur of rats resembles anything human?"

"The portion of my humanity I wish to keep isn't cleanliness," he told her, "It is my conscience."

"Why can't you keep your precious conscience intact and drink the blood of criminals?" she asked. She pushed strands of black hair from her green eyes, her beauty enticed even more of Adhemar's leftover humanity. "Why not try that instead of life like…this?"

"Because I cannot control myself unless there is six feet of soil between mortals and myself, my sweet. Because who wants to suck on the sour blood of hardened criminals when the sweet candy-like blood of children roils within young flesh?" He coughed harshly. "Such temptation is more than I can withstand!"

"So...return to your rats, Adhemar," she told him sadly and shook her head. "You are a former prince and lorded over a fiefdom thousands of years ago. You were proud once, served by knights and barons alike, fancied by beautiful maidens and envied by your enemies."

She pulled him from his grave and bit his neck. Surprise filled him. He wasn't surprised that she bit him—the temptress who had turned him into a vampire always vied to bring him out of soil. The surprise came from how much the land had changed above him. Gone was the tiny cathedral across the street. Gone were the cobblestone roads and hamlets north of the graveyard. Black paved roads separated townhouses and condominiums, called to him with the fresh scent of human blood almost too strong to resist.

"Come with me, my former lover," she purred. "And I will love you with supernatural delights!"

He pushed her away and crawled back into his grave, the soil above him sealed and smoothed over his body, and grass grew almost instantly—such was the effect upon soil whenever any vampire entered the ground. Adhemar felt guilty for breaking the trust and bond between Clarice and him, but he knew he would feel worse if he followed her to slaughter amongst the sheep of the world.

Now in the grave, the stench of sewer from below mixed with his own dead flesh, he longs to be free. How foolish he is, he thinks! Adhemar had felt if he held onto the sacredness of life, if he fought to never kill, God would save him from his vampiric curse. He knows that is fallacy now.

The coffin lid opens easily enough, and soil seems like sand in a child's sandbox, easily pushed aside as his supernatural strength gives him right of passage from the grave. He stands tall under a full moon.

"I am here, Clarice," he tells her. Adhemar wonders where she is at that exact moment. Would she smile at him? He must see what he looks like before presenting himself to her. He needs a mirror.

Across the street is a shopping mall. Another surprise. He turns to mist and sinks beneath the front door, and turns to dead flesh again on the other side. Cold eyes sink into the shadows and capture everything without the need of light. Racks of clean clothes surround him. The sign near the back reads "changing room", and three full length mirrors angle to reveal a patron's image if one stands in the proper spot. Adhemar steps up.

He no longer looks human. Fur lines his face and long whiskers jut from his cheeks. Instead of twin incisors, he has sharp fangs which protrude from his lipless mouth—how could he not have known? The face of a wharf rat stares back at him from the mirror with beady eyes.

"Dear God!" He cries and falls to his knees. "I thought you would save me from becoming a monster! Instead you allowed me to become that which I feared!"

A door unlocks at the back of the shop. A conical light pierces darkness. The silhouette behind the light reveals an angular cap—security guard. Adhemar reels with vicious anger. The light falls upon him. "Put your hands where I can see them!" Adhemar raises his hands and smiles, his rat-face grins grotesquely in the glare of human revelation. The security guard falls to his knees and wretches. Adhemar falls to his knees and feeds. Already he begins to feel more human with the taste of mortal blood.

When he finishes he sings in a childlike voice, "You are what you eat from your head to your feet."

He cackles like a hen and runs an index finger over his teeth. They're all still pointed. The mirror shows he still looks the same. His laughter fades to mournful silence. How many mortals must he suck dry before he begins to look…human again?

Adhemar exits the clothing store and looks for someone else, someone to take away his monstrous features, someone sweet and innocent, with sugar-coated blood to remove the foolishness of ever having believed God would save him.

"Only I can save myself," he mutters while spying an orphanage down the street.

THE END

Insanity
By Alexzan Burton

Don't be fooled by their disguises,
Don't ever look into their eyes

Their mangled spirits and
Tortured souls
Will swallow you whole.

Like standing in an empty room
But you feel the eyes all over you

You cannot tell where it is coming from
But you can feel them approaching.

Ever nearer, they are closing in
They want your soul,
Don't let them win.

See them, there?
Against the wall.

No where to go,
No where to fall.

They look to each other,
They point right at you
They are getting closer
And you cannot move...

As they close in, you begin to shake.
You cannot breath,
You feel your sanity quake.

They are inside your head now,
You see what they see
The pain is overwhelming
And you can't even scream...

You sit on the floor, they are standing all around
Your head hangs low
No one makes a sound

Suddenly you are screaming
Forced against the wall,
The spirits are demeaning,
You break and then fall.

They have stolen your spirit.
Your body and your soul
And left you a shell,
An empty black hole.

Now you are one of them...
Starving for souls.
Waiting in shadows,
For those who are whole.

Pick them apart,
Piece by piece
Rape their mind
Until they cease.

No longer fighting you,
You have one the game.
One more tortured soul
Alone and untamed.

You sit in waiting,
In agony, in pain.
Your screaming never ceases
Yet all goes in vain.

No one can help you,
No one can care.
You are just another demon
Though still unaware.

You shouldn't have let
Their disguises fool you.

You shouldn't have looked in their eyes.

Now you are one of them...
Condemned to all hell.
Alone for eternity,
In your empty shell

The Last Minute
By Kelly James

It was as if her soft voice and warm, inviting smile that made it all worth it. The simple touch of her hands on his shoulders and neck seemed to drive whatever demons had followed him through the door away with a power that whispered hints of near god like intensity. Above all though, was her kiss. The little kiss she planted first on his lips, then his creased brow, with all the love and tenderness that made him feel enclosed in an envelope of security and warmth, where none of the outside world's teeth could get at him.

All of these things made walking through the door every workday worth it for Vince Brady. Just seeing Sharon standing in the kitchen with her long auburn hair draped over each shoulder like folds of silk spilling from her angelic face, and her bright smile enhancing her already hypnotic green eyes to an almost euphoric state, brightened his day.

It tore Vince's heart out that tonight, while she slept, he was going to take her life.

Vince Brady was a typical man and the most extraordinary thing about him was his lovely wife Sharon. However, despite his aurora of normality, Vince Brady harbored dark and terrible secrets of a supernatural kind.

At age forty-two, Vince should be planning and looking forward to the *golden years* that he'd spend with his wife until the good Lord called them home. But he gave away that future twenty years ago when he agreed to harbor a witch.

Had he known then what he knew now, Vince considered he'd still probably make the deal. Despite always knowing, eventually, he'd have to end the arranged marriage one way or another, Vince thought it all worth it. The time he spent with Sharon—his Sharon, not the thing she was going to become if she lived until morning—had been the greatest period in his life. As with all good things, Vince knew, they never lasted long enough.

***

It was shortly after college Vince had first heard the rumors. They, the rumors, circulated among the fraternities on campus hinting of beautiful women in dire need of young husbands were willing to do *anything* to acquire said husbands. Vince and his best friend, Don Remashaw, neither very lucky in the dating department, sought out the source of these rumors.

The search took them to the small town of White Rock situated about forty-five minutes from Columbus in the heart of Ohio farmland. White Rock wasn't much different than a hundred other Ohio small towns; brick sidewalks, old buildings that didn't appear in slightest bit structurally sound, and the token Civil War statue positioned in the middle of the town beneath the traffic light, obviously put there before traffic and common sense were a concern. After a bit more investigating, Vince and Don learned, the women they sought were located in a large farmhouse on the outskirts of the quaint little village.

The outskirts of town turned out to be roughly ten miles into the farmlands.

As they pulled into the unpaved drive of a deprived looking old house surrounded by miles of bean and cornfields, Vince felt a slight wave of fear pass through deep inside of him as the scent of rot and decay surrounded him despite the lush, lonely fields of crops on each side of the property. He wasn't sure if it was the house or the loneliness of the fields that bothered him, both seemed equally ominous.

The Victorian house sat nestled back against the cornfields with only a moderate sized yard in front, apparently, the home's residents didn't deem it worth mowing judging by the waist high weeds. The house's paint had long ago yielded to the years of sun, rain, and snow and now, only flakes of white littered the weathered gray siding.

Vince parked in front of the garage—that was really just the remnants of an old barn—and both he and Don sat silently staring at the house.

"I guess this is the place," Don spoke, but his attention appeared captured by the ruined house.

"Guess so."

Both young men exited the car and stood gazing at the old house, unsure how to proceed. Vince was struck by a seemingly inordinate amount of cats roaming the environs. The animals all appeared to be watching both men with eyes that looked far too intelligent and suspicious for barn felines.

"Should we knock?" Vince asked with a shrug. However, what to say to whom ever answered the door, Vince didn't know. Vince wasn't sure, but he was sure that giving the house's occupants their true reason for being there probably wasn't the best idea.

"I don't know the place looks deserted," Don said.

Vince realized his friend was right the place did look deserted. The windows were all curtain less—some even broken and gone—and the porch roof sagged, as if at any moment it could collapse. To further the ruined, deserted look, the mailbox post leaned heavily to the right and the box itself sat atop the crooked pole, crushed and unusable.

Deciding that the entire trip was a wash, Vince motioned that they should leave when a loud fluttering sound from above startled him.

The sky darkened for an instant as a murder flew over and landed on the old house's highest gable. The crows watched the two men with interest as they pecked at the shingles roof.

Vince looked at Don and both men laughed. Vince turned back around, planning to give the birds the proverbial *bird*, but they had vanished.   Dumbfounded, he opened the car door feeling an unreasonable urge to leave, but a woman's voice calling from the direction of the house stopped him.

"Hello, young man," the voice sounded scratchy and crackled, but undeniably female.   Vince turned and was only an arms reach from the speaker.   She was an old lady, dressed in a fine gown better suited at a formal dinner than a crumbling old farmhouse.   The woman's face was crisscrossed with wrinkles and more than a couple of liver spots dotted her cheeks.   Her gray hair pulled up into an elegant bun, coupled with her robust shape, reminded Vince of Aunt May from Andy Griffith fame, but the faint stench of urine and general decay radiating from her shattered that illusion.

"Hello," Vince and Don answered in unison.

"Have you come seeking a wife?"   The old lady said with a wink and a coy smile that looked menacing on her aged faced. Despite the years, her blue eyes gleamed with a brightness that suggested an abundance of youth and vitality, giving the old lady an air of strength beyond what her age suggested.

Unsure of how to respond, Vince just gaped at the woman. Obviously reading his confusion, she clapped her two decrepit hands together vigorously.   "Of course you are!   Why else would two strapping young men be out here in the middle of nowhere?   Come in, come in, I know some pretty young girls that will be thrilled to see you!"   The ancient woman took Vince's hand and waved Don on with the other.

Her hand felt like old leather in Vince's grip as she pulled him toward the house, and it seemed to light as if dried out and lifeless, but the authority of the grip matched the intensity in her eyes.

Once inside the old house, Vince was dismayed with the condition of the interior.   Plush carpets and mirror like hardwoods covered the floors while ornate wallpaper and portraits adorned the walls.   The inside showed none of the decay that plagued the exterior. Vince discovered that looking through the windows—that looked pristine now, none even broken he could see—the front yard looked well maintained with at least a dozen different varieties of flowers blooming here and there.

More voices interrupted Vince's appraisal of the lawn. Two more ladies joined their guide, each looking so similar they could be sisters. The three crones huddled together and muttered excitedly amongst themselves for a moment before finally turning to Vince and Don.

"I am, Camilla," said the first old lady with the magnetic blue eyes. "And this is Helga and Charlotte."

Vince decided it would be easier to identify the women by the color of their dresses only smiled and offered a slight wave.

"This is a nice house. Much nicer than I expected." Don surveyed the surroundings with awe showing like a siren on his face.

"We apologize for the way the outside of our home appeared to you, young man, but we must take precautions against those that hunt us." The old woman in the Green dress said.

"Hunt you?" Vince was even more confused than before.

"You don't know?" Camilla asked placing her left hand across her breast signifying her shock at Vince's ignorance.

"I'm not even sure why we're here."

At this all three old ladies laughed heartily and then began to explain that they were witches, hunted by the government and in order for their kind to survive, they needed to place the youngest of their coven into a protected environment until their powers matured enough they could fend for themselves.

Vince listened with a crooked smile across his face. He had decided at the first mention of *witches* that the old women were insane, or at the very least, senile. He decided to play along and asked them who was it, exactly, that hunted them.

"Why the government, weren't you listening? They use the IRS and collection agencies to find us. They send in their hunters after they find us. Terrible things those hunters, I hope you never have to deal with them." Charlotte of the yellow dress stated.

"Hunters," Don asked. He was scratching his head and eyeing Vince warily.

"Wizards, warlocks, whatever you like; these men work for the government to exterminate the likes of us," Camilla's tone was grave and for the briefest of moments, Vince fancied that her eyes clouded over and then returned to their former sparkling blue.

"We're sorry to disturb you, ladies. Clearly, we've gotten the wrong address." Vince started for the door. He was feeling foolish for believing the preposterous rumors in the first place and wanted to be far away from this strange place.

"But you haven't taken a bride." One of the women from behind Vince said. Vince turned back around trying to formulate a response that wouldn't sound offensive when he saw another pair of women descending the spiral staircase.

These weren't old women though. Both newcomers looked to be just barely out of their teens and gorgeous. The first, a bubbly blonde wearing a plaid skirt and pink sweater, smiled at Don with the most inviting smile Vince had ever seen. She didn't spare Vince the courtesy of a glance.

The second young woman nearly knocked Vince off his feet by her mere presence alone. She appeared to be around the same age as the blonde, but her hair was a fiery auburn. Vince was beside himself. The woman was the girl of his dreams. It was as if he'd seen her a million times, dancing through his head while he slept or whispering sweet nothings to him while he daydreamed.

The blonde went straight to Don and seized his hand, while the auburn haired goddess took Vince's. Speechless, both men could only gawk at the women.

"Mr. Brady, this way if you please," Camilla ordered. She motioned for Vince to follow her into what looked like a parlor. "Helga will handle the arrangement with Mr. Remashaw, while we go over the specifics of your contract."

"Contract," Vince muttered, unsure if sound emitted from his mouth. He was far too enthralled with the young lady to know for sure and the fact that the old woman had used his and Don's name didn't register.

Camilla only smiled as she continued ushering Vince into the parlor. He could see Don across the room as he received the same treatment from Helga.

Camilla motioned that Vince should take a seat on the plush velvet sofa as she seated herself in a similar, high back reading chair. Vince allowed himself to be lowered on to the couch by the auburn haired beauty clutching to his arm.

"For twenty years, Sharon here will be your wife. She will accommodate you in any way you please. Whether it is a working wife, soul mate, or simply a sex toy, Sharon will comply with your every wish." Camilla said as she began unrolling a scroll that looked nearly as old as she did.

"I- I don't understand." Vince muttered, looking first at Camilla then to Sharon.

"It's simple Mr. Brady; Sharon will be your wife just as I said, for twenty years, she is yours." Camilla looked somewhat annoyed. "Perhaps, you question if she'll be satisfactory?"

"I'm just confused. Is this some kind of joke, I mean witches and warlocks?"

"This isn't a joke, Mr. Brady. Everything I have told you is true. I am a witch, and in twenty years, Sharon will be as well."

Feeling his surreal awe transforming into anger, Vince leaned back into the sofa and crossed his arms. "Prove it."

Camilla stiffened in her chair; Vince could tell she wasn't used to being challenged. She glared at him with a murderous intensity for what seemed like minutes.

Vince decided the old woman was all talk and no walk and he made to leave. Before he could pull himself off the sofa, Camilla's eyes suddenly dulled as the pupils began swirling and enlarging, engulfing the brilliant blue and mundane white completely. Serrated horns began growing from her forehead and giant bat-like wings rose from her shoulders.   Then, as if nothing had happened at all, everything about her was normal once more.

Vince could only stare wide-eyed at Camilla, unsure if what he saw was real or not. Regardless of the authenticity of the brief transformation, the fear it inspired within him was most assuredly genuine.

"Is that proof enough, Mr. Brady, or would you rather have me mount a broomstick and flutter about the room?" Camilla said, her eyes once more shining blue.

Camilla, apparently, deciding that Vince's gaping stare was an indication that he believed her to be what she claimed, continued. "Do you find Sharon an acceptable bride?"

Vince, still partially dazed with shock, slowly turned his gaze toward the beautiful Sharon. She only smiled back at him as if such exhibitions of demonic power Camilla demonstrated were commonplace. "She is perfect."

"Sharon, please provide an exhibition of your talents for Mr. Brady, while I draw his contract up," Camilla ordered. She exited the room, leaving Vince and Sharon alone.

Sharon watched the old woman leave and once the door closed behind her, Sharon stood up facing Vince. With a slight shiver, her dress slide to the floor with a whispered thud.

Despite overwhelming doubt, mingling with a fair share of trepidation, Vince felt a stirring in his groin as he looked at the nude woman. He tried to rationalize how he'd come to this point, but coming up with a logical argument that explained everything he had seen thus far wasn't forthcoming. Vince wanted answers as to why he and Donnie drove all the way out here in search of such a preposterous rumor—they normally wouldn't do such a thing. How had the house looked so deprived on the outside and so richly elegant on the inside?   But chief among his concerns was how Camilla performed her hideous transforming trick.

"We only have a few moments before Camilla returns, and there are many things I need to tell you, but promise me you won't speak of any of this to the sisters." Sharon whispered as she slowly lowered herself to her knees and rested her elbows on Vince's thighs. The stirring in Vince's groin intensified as she began methodically undoing his belt and trousers.

"What are you doing?" Vince muttered, as if he was of a mind to offer a protest to the young woman's actions, but made no effort to do so.

"She expects me to do certain *things* to ensure your cooperation. If I don't, Camilla will use other methods of persuasion. Trust me; what I do now is for both our sakes." Sharon said as she held Vince's erect penis in her hand. She leaned her face in closer to his genitals, but she spoke instead of what Vince's penis wanted.

"Everything Camilla has said is true. We are witches, and we are hunted, but not at the ferocity she'd have you believe." Sharon whispered as she slowly stroked Vince's member.

"It would be a lot easier for me to listen if you weren't doing that," Vince said. His face had flushed, and his heartbeat felt like thunderclaps in his chest.

Sharon's worried visage faded and replacing it was a sly smile. "I'm sorry, but she'll expect... certain results when she returns. Now please listen carefully, we don't have much time."

Sharon explained that witches, real witches, were women partnered with a demon. This partnership allowed the demons to exist on this plane of reality, which they were unable to do without a human host. Likewise, the witches gained access to powers undreamed of by mere humans with the union. Sharon didn't want any part of the life of a witch she told Vince, but her choice had little to do with her current situation.

Camilla and the other sisters, Charlotte and Helga, were far too powerful to resist, but Sharon explained that she had a plan and to pull it off, she'd need Vince's cooperation.

Vince was still struggling with the whole scenario and told Sharon as much.

"Please, just do what I ask, and the final proof you'll need will soon be shown." Sharon pleaded her stormy green eyes on the verge of tears.

"Alright," Vince gasped as quietly as he could. Despite all the revelations and discussions of demonic crones, he was dangerously close to orgasm. "What's… your… plan?"

As Sharon quickened the strokes of her hand-job, she laid out the specifics on what Vince must do.

"Once you sign the contract, Camilla will wipe my memory and implant new ones for the duration of our *marriage*. When our time together is over, you *cannot* allow me to return to the sisters." Sharon said as she brought Vince to climax with her touch. With her free hand, she slipped a small glass vial into Vince's hand. He looked at her questioningly, but said nothing.

"Before I am taken, twenty years from now, certain memories will stir within me hours before the demons arrival. I'm told that this is to make ready myself for the vile things entrance. And if you are trying to prevent it, I will know. So make damned sure I'm not in any condition to stop you."

Vince, heard her words, but too entranced with her hands work to make an audible reply, only nodded.

"I don't want that… that thing inside me. They say the demon only uses us indirectly to accomplish whatever goals it has in mind in this realm; like a vessel perhaps.
But I've seen some of the coven after the hunters find them. They don't kill us, as the crones would have us believe. The hunters merely exorcise the demon from the witch, leaving her powerless and mortal again. But has I've said, I've seen the crones after the demon is gone, and there is nothing left but a babbling, mindless thing. I don't want

to be lost like that, my mind devoured by such a foul creature."

Despite his near euphoric state, Vince somehow summoned pity to the forefront of his mind. Erupting with a moan of ecstasy, followed by a sigh of weary pleasure, Vince promised himself that he'd do whatever he could to help this girl. He couldn't fathom what circumstances led Sharon to this moment, but he sensed warmth in her. She didn't belong with the likes of Camilla, Helga, and Charlotte. He wasn't entirely sure as to the authenticity of the stories told from both Camilla and Sharon, and the thought of power gained using demons seemed irrational and ridiculous, belonging more on the pages of a Lovecraftian horror story than reality. However, after everything he had witnessed, Vince couldn't find it within him to outright deny the witches claims.

"Excellent!" Camilla's scratchy voice filled the room suddenly as she appeared from seemingly nowhere in front of Vince and Sharon. She was holding a stack of papers in one hand and an antique feather quill in the other. "I trust you're satisfied with Sharon's skill?"

Vince could only offer a weary smile.

"I'll take that as a yes," Camilla said. She plunged the writing end of the quill into the exposed flesh of Vince's inner thigh.

Vince shrieked in pain and made to stop Camilla's hand has it twisted the quill violently in his leg, but his body refused to move. He was paralyzed.

"Relax Mr. Brady, simple ink will not due for contracts of this type."

Camilla handed the contract and quill to Sharon and then with a withered and wrinkled finger reached and swirled a glob of the semen on Vince's lap. She jabbed the finger into the bleeding hole on his thigh. Camilla withdrew her blood and semen drenched finger and held it close to her wrinkled face, inspecting it.

"This will bind her to you, for the duration of the contract," she stuck the finger with the semen on it in Sharon's mouth and swished it around like a toothbrush. Camilla then took the quill and contract back from Sharon and turned once again to Vince. "Sign here."

Vince, feeling freedom returning to his limbs, took the contract warily. It was written in a language he didn't understand. "I can't read this."

Camilla smiled, and with a wave of her hand, the foreign letters danced and shifted

Vince watched the contract rewrite itself in horror. He no longer doubted any of the claims Camilla and Sharon made.

"Sign it, Mr. Brady," Camilla demanded.

"Sign it Vince," Sharon pleaded.

***

Vince watched as Sharon made her routine nightcap and then went to the bathroom leaving her whiskey sour unattended on the kitchen counter.

Waiting until he heard the shower come to life, Vince produced a small vial of nearly invisible liquid he'd carried with him for twenty years. He tiptoed into the kitchen. He didn't know what the mysterious liquid was and didn't care. He trusted Sharon—the real Sharon.

A sleeping drug, Vince assumed. He emptied the vial's contents into Sharon's whiskey sour. He was also acutely aware of her warning those many years ago, that a few hours before the change was to take place, she'd subconsciously begin making preparations. Vince reasoned any suspicious activity on his part might alert whatever forces at work within his wife to his intentions, so he felt it necessary to be extra cautious at this late stage.

For several months prior, Vince had searched in every magic shop, occultist, fortuneteller and new age bookstore he could find for an answer to what it was he was supposed to do. Most of the sages spouted nonsense such as he needed to *tune* himself into the universe and seek his answers there. Bullshit of course, but Vince tried the suggestion anyway, as any rational, desperate man would.

With Occultism failing to provide answers, Vince turned to religion. A complete failure on that front also. It wasn't until Vince, dejected, weary, and hopeless, wondered into a rundown biker bar in the seedy area of town that someone gave him the slightest inkling of guidance.

"I'd kill her." The burly man with an unkempt beard and absurdly long ponytail said after Vince slurred the entire story to him over several *Bud* tallboys.

"Kill her?" Vince asked as he slowly twisted the beer bottle in his hand. Hearing the two words come out of his mouth seemed vaguely comforting. Whether he spoke it as a question or a statement, he couldn't say.

"Yeah, kill her. If everything you said were true, you'd be doing the chick a favor. Live free or die, right?" The burly biker pounded the remaining beer in his bottle and slammed it back to the bar.

Leaving the bar that night, half drunk and brimming with renewed hope, was when Vince first decided that killing his wife was the right thing to do. He loved Sharon, but he'd made a promise to her a long time ago. The thought of her looking, smelling, and worst of all, being like Camilla and the sisters bothered him more than the image of her dead and decaying in the grave.

However, imagining and fantasizing about murder was a completely different animal than actually following through with the grim business. Now, the time at hand, Vince felt his nerve threatening to slither away like a frightened snake.

The shower stopped its splattering and splashing. Vince heard Sharon humming a *George Strait* song as she towel-dried her hair. Making sure her whiskey sour was in the same spot she'd left it, Vince returned to his recliner and made as if he were torn between programs by channel surfing with the remote. He noticed Sharon's shadow pass beside him and turned to look. She was gone from the bathroom and the bedroom light shone on the hallway floor.

So it begins, Vince thought as he leaned back in his *lazy boy* and settled on an episode of *The Sopranos*. The clock above the television read eleven, so if the contract proved to be accurate, Vince had another four hours left with his Sharon. He had no reason to doubt the integrity of the contract, everything thus far had been to the promised letter, and if the witches said three a.m., Vince could count on three a.m.

When you're planning murder, time seems frozen and forgotten, Vince thought as he tried not to watch the clock. He tried to distract his mind from the ugly business ahead, but he couldn't conjure a subject with the magnetism to accomplish such a feat. He kept finding his thoughts drifting more to the *how* he was going to steal Sharon's life away. In truth, Vince hadn't put much thought into what way he'd commit murder, and it was a question that needed answered and answered soon.

Drugs, of course were an option, but Vince doubted their effectiveness on a demon. No, instincts told him that something more primeval would be necessary, something involving blades and blood. Don Remashaw shot his bride to death with a .38, but Vince felt that Sharon was far too advanced for lead and gunpowder to do the trick. But as Don did, Vince thought a bullet to his brain afterwards might be a welcome end.

"Who's *Tony Soprano* screwing this week?" Sharon asked as she entered the living room and settled into her usual spot on the couch with her nightcap in hand.

"Oddly enough, his wife," Vince said. "What were you doing in the bedroom?"

"I wasn't in the bedroom; I just got out of the shower and dried my hair."

Vince felt the shorthairs on his neck stand at attention. This was really happening. She was really going to be invaded by a demon, and he was really going to murder his wife of twenty years based on that supernatural fact. Vince had felt despair many times in his life, but never at the magnitude he now felt. He wished he'd never existed at all so that fate could spare him these last few hours of cruelty. Oblivion seemed a much brighter option than his future appeared to promise.

He wanted to throw himself on Sharon and smother her with kisses and pledges of his love, but he couldn't do that. He could only try to act natural and let Sharon watch *The Sopranos*, ignorant of what fate awaited her at the hands of the only person in the world she loved and trusted.

"I thought I heard you go in there is all," Vince mumbled disinterested.

Before *Tony Soprano* went off the air, Sharon proclaimed she didn't feel well and retreated to the bedroom. Vince had a sudden flash of hope, maybe the contents of the vial wasn't sleeping drugs after all. Maybe it'd been poison and Sharon had saved him from the vile job by, in essence, killing herself twenty years ago. However, it wasn't to be.

Vince flipped through the channels for a while longer, before going to the bedroom. He wanted to spend as much time as possible with Sharon—his Sharon—before the time came, but anything he did out of the ordinary could alert the monster within her.

Vince lay in bed, pretending sleep as he suffered the cruelest misery imaginable. The thought of oblivion crossed his mind again.

Don had it backwards; he should have killed himself first.

Vince dismissed the thought. If he committed suicide, Sharon was still condemned.

Vince decided he was going to be a man and do what had to be done.

***

The digital clock on the nightstand next to Vince boldly proclaimed it was two fifty-one a.m. and Sharon still drew breath in smooth, even repetitions.

Vince, however, lay beside her; sticky with cold sweat and his fingers numb from the death grip he held on a kitchen knife hidden beneath his pillow. He had to act now. If the sleeping drugs lasted long enough to keep her under another hour or so, Vince had a good idea the sisters would come looking for their new edition. Dealing with Camilla and her lot wasn't something Vince wanted to do.

Besides, he doubted even the magically enhanced drug possessed enough power to restrain Sharon once she was with the demon.

No, he would do it now, before the demon came or Sharon woke.

Kneeling beside Sharon, knife hovering over her heart, Vince hesitated, as he looked at her sweet, innocent face peaceful in sleep. He wondered if Don hesitated before he shot his bride and then turned the gun on himself. Vince doubted it; Don
Remashaw apparently possessed more strength than he could even imagine. But Don was gone and was of no help to Vince now. Alone with only Sharon, a serrated kitchen knife, and precious little time, Vince felt a tear trickle down his cheek and then another.

Two fifty-seven a.m.

With tears flowing freely, Vince raised the knife high above his head and drove it downward with all his might. One stroke, he thought, and it's over.

The instant before the jagged blade should have found soft flesh, Sharon's eyes flashed wide and a vise-like grip stopped his hand in mid thrust. The last images Vince saw before darkness claimed him were of Sharon's face; twisted into a nightmarish version of its former self. Her emerald green eyes disappeared behind a black cloud, and her angelic smile vanished into a maelstrom of wicked fangs. This is how it ended for Vince Brady.

***

The demon Contuca howled with delight as it flicked the fragments of skull and brain matter off its flesh vessel's fingers. The night was a victory, but only with the smallest of margins. The flesh vessels seemed to be growing more intolerant of Contuca and her peers' powers of possession with each passing season.

"You cut that close sister." Camilla's scratchy voice sounded from the dark recesses of the bedroom where Contuca knew she'd been waiting, unable to interfere or effect the situation in anyway.

Every game has its rules, Contuca thought as she turned toward her sister.

"The flesh vessel provided the male with an old world magic that very nearly caused my doom!" Contuca growled as she kicked the headless corpse of Vince Brady.

"Well, the balance insists that these creatures get a fair opportunity to save their selves one time before the twenty year possession begins. You knew that, and it seems you came away the winner, congratulations, sister." Camilla said. She stepped from the darkness, taking Contuca's hand in her own and looking questionably at the alarm clock on the nightstand. "But you must tell me, how did you survive the old world magic? That spell should have bound you from any interference until the stroke of the witching hour, yet you came through with a minute to spare."

"Yes the old world magic proved paralyzing, but the fool waited all this time before finally giving the flesh vessel the spell only hours ago. Smelling something amiss, I acted." Contuca shrugged with her rapidly slumping and aging shoulders. Some day, she hoped, they'd find a stronger race more capable of sustaining a demon, but for now, she was pleased with her flesh vessel.

Camilla regarded her with raised brows. "Pray tell sister."

"I set the clock back a minute."

The End

THE HOOKUP
By Mark Jackson

Angelina scanned the room. The pulsing white light flashed in her eyes, causing her pupils to dilate and contract with the thumping beat of the music. She knew she could find the kind of man she desired, and it wouldn't take much time to do it.

Club 59 was a South Beach hot spot for the beautiful people mostly in their twenties, but that wasn't Angelina's target audience. It was men in their forties, sometimes even older, that suited her needs.

Wasting no time, she strutted across the dance floor towards the pink neon-lit bar that curved out in a horseshoe shape on the far end of the club. In seconds, she knew she had drawn the attention of every male in the room as well as those of most females, just as she had intended. The Prada cocktail dress emphasized her firm c-cup breasts, tiny waist and the swell of her hips to perfection. Its color set off her olive, flawless complexion and black flowing hair, while the high hemline stressed her long shapely legs. She stopped in the middle of the floor and bent over to adjust a strap on one of her Franco Sarto shoes. She glanced at the nearby men, their eyes staring hungrily at her butt, hoping to see just a little bit more.

With a smile that took in her audience, she proceeded to the bar and leaned her back against it, thrusting her pelvis out invitingly. The six foot, pink '59' glowing above her gave her the supernatural look of an angel, which couldn't have been farther from the truth. Then, as if on cue, a man approached.

"Do you mind if I buy you a drink and get your autograph? I'll keep it discrete so no one will bother you." Angelina turned to see a young good-looking guy, with thick, brown hair and dark skin holding out a napkin and pen. Angelina glanced at the napkin then back at the man who was now flashing her an Abercrombie and Fitch model smile. She knew this was just another attempt at a pickup line, but she played along willingly enough.

"My autograph?" Angelina produced a confused smile.

"You are Eva Longoria aren't you?" the man asked, trying on a confused smile of his own.

Angelina had to admit this line wasn't too bad, and she did resemble Eva Longoria only about six inches taller, but young unmarried men weren't what she was looking for. What she was looking for was... him. She had turned back to scan the crowd and had been looking at the rail that separated the dance floor from the rest of the bar when she saw him. The rail was a favorite spot for the guys either too embarrassed or too old to mix it up with the twenty something's on the dance floor, and they always lined up there like birds on a wire.

Angelina looked back at the good-looking guy who was still holding out the napkin and pen. "Nice try, but you're not my type." She turned and walked out on the dance floor, while behind her, she heard the good-looking guy saying something about how he could be whatever type she wanted, but within a few steps, the pounding beat of 50 Cent drowned out all other sounds. Angelina headed towards a stunning blonde wearing a dress just as tight, but even shorter than hers.

***

"Damn, Elliott, this music sucks!" Jim said, yelling to be heard over the music blasting out of the six-foot JBL speakers that surrounded the dance floor like black skyscrapers.

Elliott, a well-built and attractive forty-year-old electrical engineer from central Ohio, just smiled at Jim and took another long drink of his Coors Light.

"You, my friend, are correct, but do you see that Latino babe?" Elliott asked, nodding towards the dance floor where a twenty-something woman with a killer body and long black hair was grinding with a blond woman almost as good looking. "And, I think she's checking me out." He took another drink and leaned on the rail.

"Oh, momma!" Jim said. He joined Elliot on the rail and watched the two women. The Latino was in the process of rubbing herself up and down the leg of the blonde to the wild encouragement of every guy within shouting distance.

"I'm in love," Elliott said.

"In lust is more like it," Jim countered.

Elliott sighed, thinking of his wife and kids some 1200 miles away in Ohio. However, this was South Beach and what happens in South Beach stays in South Beach. *After all,* Elliott reminded himself, *I'm not looking for a relationship so it really isn't cheating anyway.* He sighed again and was about to head back to the bar when the Latino looked directly at him and ran her pink, wet tongue over her perfect white teeth. Elliott about dropped his bottle.

"Did you see that?" Elliott elbowed Jim in the ribs. "I told you she's checking me out."

"Are you sure it wasn't someone behind you?" Jim asked. "Nothing personal, but it's a little hard to imagine a hot woman like that checking you out." Jim finished the remaining half of his beer and belched.

"Thanks for the confidence, buddy." Elliott pulled a twenty out of his pocket and handed it to Jim. "After that comment, I shouldn't buy you a beer, but I'm not leaving this spot, and I know you won't go buy the beers just because you're a nice guy."

"I'm hurt," Jim said, grabbing the twenty from Elliott then disappearing into the crowd.

Elliott looked back at the women. His heart rate went up when the Latino looked at him again. His mind filled with visions of a night with her, pushing out any lingering thoughts there may have been of his wife. Things started to stir to life in regions much lower than his brain, but Elliott didn't notice, and really didn't care: the chance of a lifetime loomed on the horizon like an afternoon thunderstorm.

50 Cent finished, and The Pussycat Dolls picked up with 'Don't Cha', keeping the pounding beat pulsating through the crowd like an ancient mating ritual. The Latino leaned over to say something to the blonde, and they both looked toward Elliott. The blonde said something back, and they both laughed before the Latino started walking towards Elliott.

You have to be shitting me Elliot thought as the woman approached. The closer she got, the better she looked. He suddenly wished he had beer to down for the boldness needed to deal with a woman like this. There had to be a catch; there always was. Maybe they were laughing at him and this was all just a big joke, or a bet, or-

"Why aren't you out on the floor dancing? You look like you are in pretty good shape." She ran her eyes over Elliott's chest then glanced down at his left hand. Elliott followed her glance and saw she was looking at his wedding ring. He couldn't believe he'd forgotten to take it off before they got to the club.

"Well, I'm not really that good of a dancer. I hardly ever come in to a club like this," Elliott lied. He wasn't a good liar and he was sure he was going to blow this. He thought of a hunter hiding in the brush, and then sneezing just as a trophy buck entered the clearing.

"Really?" She arched perfect eyebrows set above the darkest, most beautiful eyes Elliott had ever seen in his life. "I don't either. So what do you say we get out of here and go someplace a little quieter?" She reached up, put her hand on Elliott's arm, and gave it a gentle squeeze.

Elliott couldn't believe this was happening. He had never had a woman even close to this caliber hit on him before. Fat, ugly, or more likely both, wasn't too unusual, but a woman that looked like she could be featured on the cover of Cosmopolitan? No way. He looked around for Jim, but he was nowhere in sight. Elliott didn't want to just leave without saying anything, but he wasn't going to take the chance that while he was off hunting down Jim, little Miss Latino would come to her senses.

"Yeah, I do want to get out of here," Elliott said. "But I-"

"Stop," she said staring into Elliott's eyes. "If you're going to tell me you rode with your friend so you don't have a car, that's fine. I'll drive. And if you're going to tell me you're married, I know and I don't care. I'm not looking for a relationship, I'm just looking for a little fun. Now let's go." She stepped through an opening in the rail, took Elliott's hand, and led him towards the club exit.

Elliott prayed he wouldn't wake up from what had to be a dream. He took one last look over his shoulder for Jim, not so much to let him know he was leaving, but to gloat about whom he was leaving with. However, with still no sign of him, Elliott quickly shifted his mental gears from gloating to mentally practicing his patented bedroom moves he would be blessing this beautiful woman with in the very near future.

***

Her apartment was nothing like what Elliott thought it would be. It was in an older section of South Beach he had never been to before and probably would have avoided had he known about it. To get in, they walked up a narrow set of steps to a small landing that had a door off to either side. Somewhere in the building, he could hear a baby crying, some guy calling his wife a stupid bitch, and the thump of what Elliott figured was no doubt a Latino beat. The smell of cigarette smoke oozed from the walls in sickening sheets stinging Elliott's eyes.

Although Elliott had often fantasized about picking up a woman and bragging to all his friends about it, he had never actually gone through with it. But deep down, all he really wanted to do is see if he could. He did love his wife, but things were pretty dull at the home front, especially in bed.

He was just starting to think this wasn't such a good idea when the woman suddenly dropped her keys and bent over in front of him, giving him a titillating view up her short skirt and extinguishing his virtuous thoughts like a match in a windstorm.

After she picked up the keys, she looked over her shoulder and gave Elliott a knowing smile, then proceeded to unlock the door and step into the apartment.   Elliott, heart pounding with excitement, followed her in. As soon as he stepped through the door, he saw the inside was a perfect match for the outside.

The only light was provided by a small table lamp in the opposite corner, which barely illuminated the cheap looking furniture spread around the room. But worse than the uninviting atmosphere was the smell. It reminded Elliott of a trip he had made to the zoo with the kids last summer, but the zoo didn't have the underlying smell of something rotten. He thought maybe a rat or something had-

"By the way, my name is Angelina," the woman said interrupting Elliott's thoughts.

At first, Elliott didn't even notice her extended hand, but then quickly took it. "I'm Elliott. It's real nice-"

"Let's just cut through the bullshit and get down to why we are here," Angelina said, pulling her hand out of Elliott's and pushing him against the wall.

Before Elliott could protest, which was the farthest thing from his mind, she pressed her lips against his and slid her tongue deep in his mouth. Her breath was hot and sweet and Elliott had never experienced such passion. She was literally ripping his shirt off and pressing herself against him with such force, that it almost hurt. Almost.

She reached down beside him and released a door Elliott hadn't even noticed was there. As soon as the door opened, the zoo smell became stronger, but the fact Angelina was already pulling off his belt put the importance of what the room smelled like right up there with what time the next rerun of I Love Lucy might be on. Keeping her mouth locked with his, she backed him into the room and pushed the door closed behind them.

The room was pitch black, and as soon as the door closed, all sounds from the surrounding apartments ceased. Even the sound of the door closing was a muffled thump, but like the smell, these thoughts were nothing more than sparks flashing through Elliott's mind as Angelina pulled off his pants and moved him deeper into the room.

"Where are we?" Elliott panted.

"Shhhh," Angelina said, pressing her finger to his lips.

Elliott couldn't remember ever being so worked up in his life. There was something about Angelina that was different from any other woman he had been with. It was like her need was so deep she could barely contain herself. This animal desire was contagious, and Elliott found himself losing all thoughts other than he needed this woman now.

The back of Elliott's legs hit something and he fell into what felt like a large wooden chair. He moved his hands instinctively down to catch himself, and felt the large flat arms of the chair. The seat and back felt sticky, like something had been previously spilled on it. His next sensation was of cold steel clasps snapping over his wrists.

"Hey what's this?" Elliott asked into the dark. He had never been with a woman that was into this kind of action, but wasn't really surprised that Angelina was.

"Shhhh," Angelina said again. "Relax and enjoy the ride."

By the sound of her voice, Elliott could tell her position was a littler lower than his, then he felt two more clasps snap shut, one over each ankle. Then she was on top of him and wasted no time in consummating the evening. He could tell she still had her dress on, but that was it. What he saw under her skirt on the steps, or more what he didn't see, was now confirmed.

Her heat was close to feverish, and it felt like he had just been immersed in hot, wet velvet. The feeling of helplessness was intoxicating. At first, he was a little nervous about it, but the fact there was nothing he could do to stop her, or slow her down even if he wanted to, somehow made it even more intense than he could have ever imagined. Elliott took short labored breaths, and he could feel his lips getting numb. This was the most incredible sex of his life. It was in this deepest moment of desire he knew he had to have Angelina more than just one night. He needed to have her again and-

A clicking noise suddenly sounded from somewhere behind him. The noise sounded familiar, but Elliott couldn't quite place it.

Then, without ceremony, Angelina stopped gyrating on Elliott's lap and climbed off.

"What are you doing?" Elliott gasped, not believing she was actually stopping now when he was only moments away from...

The rapid clicking sound started again, and this time the image of a set of plastic teeth, chattering their way across a gag shop countertop, flashed in his mind. Click, click, click, click, click, click. "And what is that clicking?"

Elliott wasn't able to turn in the direction of the sound, but the room was so black that even if he could, it would be like trying to see the bottom of a swimming pool filled with ink. Then he heard something else: A voice from the direction of the clicking that made his body go as rigid as a day old corpse, and his penis to wilt like a delicate flower.

"Yeah, yeah, yeah, chop, chop, chop, chop, ohh, oooohh," the voice said from the darkness.

The weird acoustics of the room made the voice sound flat and distant. It sounded human, or at least somewhat human, but not like anything, or anyone, Elliott had ever heard before.

"Who's there?" Elliott yelled, suddenly realizing the vulnerability of being strapped securely in a chair in a totally dark room... naked. He jerked his hands, but the cold steel bit into his wrists, sending searing pain through his arms. His eyes widened in the blackness and sweat started pushing through his pores in waves.

"Ohhhh, oh, chop, chop, chop, chop, yeah, yeah, ohhhh, chop."

The voice now sounded closer, and Elliott thought he could hear a kind of wet slapping sound.

"Let me out of this chair. Let me out of this chair now!" He jerked harder, but the straps held fast, and chair didn't move, suggesting it had been bolted to the floor. Elliott's heart pounded so hard that it made dull thumping sounds in his ears. He felt disoriented; could feel himself spinning downward into a darkness even more impenetrable than the blackness of the room.

"Oh calm down," Angelina said. He heard a snap and suddenly the room filled with a brilliant white light, saving him from blacking out, but forcing him to close his eyes, then slowly open them against the glare.

As his eyes started to adjust, he found himself in a large room, the walls and ceilings of which were covered with some kind of white, billowed fabric that, even in his frantic state, Elliott registered as the cause of the deadened sound. Strange, maroon smears and splatters covered the walls and floor like someone had thought decorating the room by smearing red paint on the walls would add a nice touch to the room's appeal. What looked like a large bone lay against one wall.

"Did you enjoy yourself?" Angelina asked.

Elliott jerked his head towards Angelina. "What the hell is going on? Let me out of this chair." Angelina just smiled at Elliott and held up something between her finger and thumb that Elliott recognized as a gold ring. He looked down at his left hand and saw his wedding ring was missing. He looked back at Angelina. "Hey, what-"

"You don't deserve to wear this anyway," she said and tossed it in what looked like a gallon sized pickle jar that was already at least half full of a variety of gold and silver rings. The dull ping it made had the finality of the sound of prison bars slamming shut on the beginning of a convicted murderer's life sentence.

"Oooooh, yeah, yeah, yeah, yip, yip, chop."

Elliott had forgotten about weird voice approaching from behind. He tried to turn again, but the back of the chair was tall enough to block any view.

"What the fuck is that!" Elliott demanded, but his quavering voice made it sound more like a whine.

"You mean who the fuck is that," Angelina responded calmly. "That is my husband, Max."

"Your husband?" Elliott squeaked, suddenly finding it difficult to breathe. The thought a man capable of making those insane gibbering noises was somewhere right behind him, sent a chill crawling across his skin like a thousand tiny spiders.

"Yes, my husband. A husband who I remained faithful too while he was a successful scientist at Rockwool Labs and still remain faithful to even through his... ah, let's say unfortunate accident at the genetics lab. For better and for worse you know." Angelina smiled at Elliott. Her dark eyes gleamed in the fluorescent glow of the overhead light. "Oh, but of course you don't know about that do you? You don't know what it's like to be faithful, even during the better side of it. You probably have a beautiful wife at home, but here you are screwing me, and you barely even know my name."

Elliott looked back at Angelina. He couldn't believe this was happening. This was just supposed to be a simple hookup. Nothing more. Just a little fun. Get in and get out with no strings attached. And how could she talk about being faithful when only two minutes ago she was riding him like a country bar mechanical bull? He was just positioning his mouth to ask her that very question when he caught movement in the corner of his eye. He looked down to his right and struggled to comprehend what he saw moving across the floor.

One bulging, blue eye stared up at him from what looked more like a cabbage than a head. The other eye was gone, leaving nothing more than a swollen pink socket. Its nose was turned up like the Phantom of the opera and its mouth was a protrusion of sharp teeth, barely contained by thin white lips. Scraggly hunks of hair trailed off its cabbage head and down its knotted back as it pulled itself along the floor by its hands. One leg pushed at the slick tile floor while the other leg, which looked more like a seal's fin, slapped at the floor in wet smacks. A blackish, blue hole was positioned on its back just above its mutated legs and was bubbling out something that looked like a mixture of blood and shit.

"Ooooooh, Ooooh, yeah, yeah, chop, chop, yip, yip, yip, yip," said the monstrosity that Angelina claimed as her husband.

"Holy shit! Let me out of here! Let me the fuck out of here! Oh please. NO!" Elliott screamed. He jerked so violently at the clasps that blood streamed down the chair in small rivers.

Max dragged himself around in front of Elliott and stared up at him with his one rolling, blue eye. His teeth chattered, making the clicking sound Elliott had heard before. Then, like a bird pecking seed, his head shot forward and he bit three toes off Elliott's right foot.

Elliott screamed in pain as Max crunched through the toes, swallowing them in a gulp before running his long, black tongue over his pointed teeth.

Angelina looked lovingly at her husband. "Now you enjoy yourself Max." She started to open the door then stopped and turned back to Elliott. "Oh, just so you know, Max is especially fond of the places I've... that I've been, so to speak." Ignoring Elliott's pleas, she turned back to the door, leaving Max to make his way up Elliott's jerking legs.

Angelina closed the door and leaned against the wall. Sometimes she did feel guilty about having sex with the unfaithful pigs she brought back to Max, but she had to test how faithful they were. There really was nothing to feel guilty about. *After all* Angelina thought *I'm not looking for a relationship, so it really isn't cheating, anyways.*

THE END

The Massacre
By Alexzan Burton

Where is your sanity
Since the massacre has begun
Where is your Jesus now?

What are you crying for?
Who is going to save you
Now that your life is done?

The pain won't last
For very much longer
It makes me stronger

Watching you suffer
Against the chains
Watching your flesh tear away

Hearing your cries,
Looking into your eyes,
Makes my suffering dissipate.

I lie at night and anticipate
The most beautiful way that you create
My most deviate fantasies

My most intimate conspiracies
A longing so diseased
To cause you pain.

To watch you fall
And lose it all

Because of me

These Human Monsters
By John Miller and Buffy Vincent

She sees everything while moving in total darkness, her eyes catching the tiniest reflections of light, and no shadow is too great to peer into save for the darkened heart of humankind. The vampire hisses as she walks across the balcony, her marble-white hand sliding smoothly over the polished baluster, her steps silent and sure. She has walked this way many times. It is her house. It is the house of her husband and her children, those beautiful vampiric beings whose fear calls to her now. They have them. The humans wait for her below at the foot of the stairs using her own children as bait.

They cannot kill her children; they are already dead. Their tiny little hearts were dead at birth and have never once beat with pulse, and though her children grow, they will never be truly alive, just as she hasn't been alive for over a thousand years. Yet does dead flesh constitute a lifeless existence? Does life have to depend upon organic flesh and living cells? Can't life be about what's inside a person's heart instead of what a person's body craves and what a person's body resembles?

Can't life be about just that: life?

While they cannot kill her children, they can make them go away. There are certain tools humans use to remove her kind from existence, and she steps into the soft glow of one of those tools: firelight. Burning below is her furniture, the expensive couch and matching chairs her husband worked so hard to purchase. They have his body now. Her husband, together with her, created the existence of their children and helped her name them Emily, Sarah and David— sweet poor David whose innocence is as bright as the noonday sun she hasn't seen in centuries.

Does it have to be like this? Do her enemies have to demand on titles and stereotypes? Of course they do—they're humans. They are pathetic lifeless humans with darkened hearts. Ken already has a wooden stake through his heart, and his head is someplace else. She watched them carry his body from the white panel-van still parked outside their house—her house now. It was a sign indicating they meant business.

When she first saw them carrying Ken's decapitated body from the van to her home, she screamed for her children to go into hiding while bloody tears streamed down her face. While vampiric children, she has still taught them stranger-danger, the product of home-schooling. The children knew to go down into the cellar and hide among the boxes of old clothes from centuries past. Somehow the humans discovered them, and now they hold her sweet children against their will, stakes aimed at their hearts, garlic—quite harmless—hanging from heads bowed in fear and shame. Samantha hears the humans scold her children for being evil, vile creatures of wickedness. They demand her children repent. Repent of what? Samantha chuckles mirthlessly, for her children have harmed none in their existence. Ken and she never taught them the ways of violence…the ways of humankind.

Now they suffer for it.

Ken works—worked—at the local emergency care facilities a couple blocks away. The doctor there knows Ken is a vampire, and he knows Ken's entire family. So much violence happens in the inner-city, and so much blood spills freely. So much, in fact, that Ken works for half the amount the doctor would pay a human, and the rest of his pay is in human blood. He receives seven dollars per hour tax-free for cleaning the office at night. The rest of his pay is in the blood bags the doctor secures for him in the large double-door refrigerator, and Ken takes the blood bags home to his family at the end of each night. In their kitchen they pop straws into the blood bags or slide their twin incisors into them, sharing the day's events and listening to

Ken talk about the remaining human patients at the medical outreach center.

"Two gang-bangers were brought in with shotgun wounds, and both died. Before that sixteen teenage mothers received prenatal instructions. A cop walked through looking for a pedophile and Dr. Gibson's zealous daughter-in-law keeps spying on me."

The story was virtually the same each night. Ken told them about the violence of the city, the torn and mangled bodies of "civilized" humans going in and out of the medical facilities. Ken always got there shortly after dusk. Ken is older than Samantha, and because he is so old he is more powerful than most vampires and can stay out during dusk and dawn without burning beneath the sun. As powerful as he is, he hasn't mastered any vampiric powers. He has always been peaceful, possessing the heart of a lover—a heart now staked through with human viciousness.

"Come down, Samantha!" Tabitha, Dr. Gibson's daughter-in-law, calls. "Or Emily here will be the first to die."

"I'm already dead, mortal!" her little girl hisses rebelliously.

Samantha hears live flesh striking dead flesh and another hiss escapes her lips. While Ken hadn't mastered his vampiric powers, she has. She is immensely powerful and could easily kill the mortal fools below—if only they did not have her beloved children.

"Harm a hair on their heads and I'll rip out your fucking hearts," she yells. She steps fully into the light and sixteen rifles aim at her chest and head. "Shoot and your lives end now."

They hesitate and their fear wafts upward in the warm currents of the room, currents mortals could never sense, but she senses them as well as their moral terror. She knows them all too well. Most vampires are peaceful creatures preferring solitude. Every once in a while a vampire will come along who is a serial killer, and it is the serial killers who give vampires a bad name. Samantha doesn't believe all mortals are evil just because some humans are serial killers; so why do the mortals believe her family is evil?

"Get thee behind me, satan!" Tabitha shouts to rally her religious troops. "No weapon formed against us shall stand."

Tabitha belongs to a non-denominational church where speaking in tongues and dancing with arms raised to Jesus is expected of all Spirit-filled believers. The parishioners of her church hold daily prayer meetings and hold signs in front of abortion clinics. They send letters to congressmen and vote, their politics defined solely by abortion-related issues. Their preacher is in prison for having helped fund the bombing of an abortion clinic in Chicago, and his son now leads the church in his father's footsteps. They lay hands on the sick and cast out demons. Alcohol; all diseases; mental problems; suicidal tendencies; adultery and fornication; and rock and roll: these are all ramifications of demonic possession in her mind and the minds of her fellow fanatic parishioners.

Samantha has existed through more than one Inquisition. She hasn't the heart to see the dawning of a new breed of hatred spawn burning fires of uncontrolled fear again. And it's all because of human darkness, something she just can't comprehend although she once was one of them.

Once she worshiped and went to Mass weekly same as everyone in her fiefdom. The barons and dukes lorded over King Aaron's kingdom—a king everyone would forget about for being most unremarkable save for the most boringly astute of historical scholars. She knows what it is to pray and believe. Hadn't she counted on God to save her when Baron Vlad sent for her? Hadn't she counted on God to save her when twin incisors slid over his smiling lips?

God hadn't answered her prayers then, and she knows she cannot count on him now. How could a God allow these human monsters into her house? How could a God allow these human monsters to live after what they did to Ken?

Up the steps Tabitha approaches, her face skewered with revulsion just as Samantha's face mirror's Tabitha's own face as she watches her approach. Samantha hisses allowing Tabitha to see her fangs. They meet beneath the chandelier at the top of the stairway, the dangling crystals reflecting firelight. Tabitha holds a miniature Bible before her along with a crucifix as if it can help.

Nothing can help Tabitha now. Samantha vows it.

"If she harms me kill the children," Tabitha shouts. The mob murmurs approval, and Samantha sees her little girls and sweet David. "Start with the youngest one first."

"Mommy!" David calls while stretching his arms toward her. Three men hold the incredibly strong four-year-old down on the floor as he struggles and weeps bloody tears. "Mommy, I need you!"

"You monsters!" she yells. "He's just a child!"

"It looks as if you are the monster, demon," Tabitha objects, "With your white skin and fanged smile."

"Just give the word, Tabitha," a man from the mob calls, "And we'll bring that demon-bitch down!"

She smiles and Samantha realizes Tabitha loves the power she wields over the mob. It was Tabitha who had discovered Ken's secret and shared it with the others, and it was she whom had orchestrated the mob—Dr. Gibson had told Ken about it several nights previous, but Ken had felt it just an ugly rumor. When he'd told Samantha about it, she had responded by saying icily, "Where there's smoke there's fire." Now there is smoke rising through her home stinging her eyes.

"Just be still and everything will be alright, sweetie," she tells David. She sees a red welt upon Emily's face. "Are you okay, honey?"

"Of course, mom," Emily replies. "I'm a vampire!"

Samantha knows Emily tries to act brave before the human monsters, and perhaps she even attempts to bluff them. Yet she knows her nine year old daughter is terrified. So is Samantha.

Twenty zealots and sixteen rifles wait below. Samantha realizes if they shoot she can easily move quick enough to pull

Tabitha before her and use her body as a shield. Some bullets may get through, but what worries her most is her children will be destroyed immediately. Just one small push into the burning couch is all it will take to remove her children from her forever. Sixteen men train rifles on Samantha, and three men hold terrified David down. The remaining man points a gun at Emily's head while keeping his arm wrapped around her neck tightly. It's tight enough to shut off her windpipe now, but Emily doesn't breathe nor does her heart beat, yet she is more fully alive than any of the human scum in attendance. The couch and chairs are in the middle of the den, and the flames are eight feet high. A video plays in the VCR and Elmo sings to a goldfish on television.

David frees himself by biting deeply into the wrist of one of the men, and when the man snatches his hand away in fear holding it, David leaps away and bounds toward the stairs. "No, David," she cries but it is too late, the damage is done, and violence echoes in the sound of rifles firing and the acrid stench of gun smoke. Samantha pulls Tabitha to her and bullets whip into Tabitha's back. Her eyes widen in surprise and Tabitha doesn't look as religious as before with dying eyes. Samantha snatches the Bible from her limp hands and shoves the tiny Bible into her mouth, then kicks out. Tabitha flies over the railing and over the mob.

"How does your God taste now?" Samantha cries. "Imagine: dead at the hands of your fellow believers who shot you."

The rifles fire again, but this time Samantha has no cover. The three wounds in her body already begin healing. One bullet went clean through her calf, and while it slows her down, it does not incapacitate her. Like a panther she soars over the volley of bullets, and before the Christians can squeeze the triggers on their rifles again, she falls before them. Her face still bloody from having cried over seeing Ken, she looks horrific... but only because the human monsters have brought this change upon her. Her children scatter, temporarily forgotten by the religious monsters. Samantha crouches by Tabitha's prone body, and she sees Tabitha's eyes staring up toward heaven, but her face does not look as though it's filled with heavenly peace, especially with the miniature Bible protruding from her puffy mouth. It makes her look like a stuffed pig with an apple in its maul.

Emily and Sarah bolt after David as he rushes upstairs. A sob catches in her throat as she sees blood trailing down David's chin and he licks his lips. He's too young to know what temptation is or how to deal with it, and she will make these mortals pay dearly for what they've done.

She whips through them, a shadow-blur moving almost faster than the flickering firelight can move, almost invisible and with preternatural ease, slicing and biting and tearing and meshing. Arms and heads fly through the air. A mental command causes the brain of one man to explode, and skull shards impale the man next to him. Guts are ripped out, and she chokes the final mortal with the intestines of his spiritual brother. She smiles—her children are safe.

She glances at the fire and worries about how fast it moves through the den. Already the curtains catch fire, and the carpeting burns toward the wall. She flings human blood from her claws counting bodies. That is when she realizes there aren't twenty bodies. She doesn't know how many there are, but it's more like fifteen or sixteen bodies. The sound of heavy footfalls from upstairs tells her where the remaining mortals are. They made good their escape from her slaughter while she'd killed their brethren just as she kept an eye on the front door in case any tried escaping or more showed. She hadn't considered them going up the stairs—don't they realize that's certain death? That's where the fire's going.

She moves up the stairs just as the flames lick the ceiling and begin moving within the interior of the wall. The heat is powerful and she resists her vampiric instincts to flee in terror—her children need her.

She does not know where her children are, nor does she know

where the human monsters are. All are silent now, hiding and lurking behind cover. Her children hide for their very existence; the human monsters hide waiting to attack.

"Stay hidden, kids," she calls.

A pop sounds loudly and a bullet whizzes at her, and she ducks beneath it and watches it trail overhead. Down the hallway a rifle disappears behind a closing door.

"Mommy!" Emily's voice rings out, but from where she doesn't know.

A door to her left is open, and it was closed when she'd just past it. In the deafening roar of the rifle, she'd failed to hear the sound of the moving door. She sniffs and smells the human oils and fear, close. The sound of metal cocking and sweaty palms slapping cold steel. She ducks again as another deafening blast rocks her senses. She sends a clawed hand backwards, and the shooter's head flies over the balcony, crashing through the crystal chandelier, and smacks wetly against the wall where it slides down to the stairs leaving a long bloody smear.

Sixteen, she thinks as she moves forward toward the other rifle. The doors are open in the hall and the heat of the fire is searing behind her, crawling over the ceiling and up the stairs. She has to find her children and get out.

The hallway is a haze of grey smoke that burns her eyes as she tries in vain to see down it. She hears a soft ruffle and the slide of a closet door to her right in Sarah's pink princess bedroom.

"Get in," a whisper says and shuffling feet on carpeting hits her ears. If she had a heart it would thud in her chest, her children are safe from the monsters, hidden away in a large closet. She crouches now as she moves away from the door and hopes she hasn't betrayed their hiding place by lingering too long in the hall.

Her mind awash with the horrors of the night is beginning to snap, her powers roar and the need to taste more blood, to finish her vengeance makes the fangs in her mouth ache. A rifle muzzle moves down the hall, a dark line in the smoke-filled hall. She mentally pulls the gun from the hands that hold it and tosses it away. A shout emanates from the human monster wielding it. She sees his body appear; it's all she needs.

Samantha shoots down the hall with the preternatural speed of her kind, claws slicing through soft human flesh and fangs ripping and tearing, as hot blood gushes over her face and shirt. She hears a sound and turns to find number eighteen standing behind her, gun hanging loose in the woman's hand. With a roar she attacks taking the woman to the floor in one fluid movement. She gouges at the eyes and rips open the throat. Samantha leaves the woman to writhe and die on the floor, the pristine white carpet forever stained crimson beneath her feet.

"Mommy?" cries David's small voice from the hallway. "Mommy where are you?"

She rushes through the room, back the way she came, blood and gore dripping from her body. As she enters the hall she hears the crack of a gun and she watches as her precious son's eyes bulge. Blood seeps slowly out of his mouth, his eyes roll up in his head and she see in slow motion the horror of her son falling dead at her feet, the back of his head a mesh of hair and blood—her sweet David.

Pain slices through her and rage tinges her vision red as she flies down the hall cutting down the rest of the humans in her path. Nineteen and twenty die quickly in heaps of tangled flesh, bone and blood.

The fire burns at her feet, her shoes hot with licking flames, flames scorching her skin and singing her long hair, flames cutting the hallway in two separating her from her children. She feels the fire eating at her legs, but she stand there and watches as it climbs the walls around her. Samantha is frozen, made immobile by the horrors that have finally penetrated her mind.

"MOMMY!" a child's voice screams and she hears her Sarah crying now from her room down the hall.

Her children! She must move. Her feet move of their own volition pushing her forward through the flames toward her daughters. She smells her skin burning and charring, but Samantha doesn't feel it. She falls into Sarah's room, just breaking the threshold and pulls her burning legs in the door. Samantha drags herself to her feet and slams the door on the flames. Somewhere the house creaks and then shutters as some piece of the building gives way.

She goes directly to the closet and rips the door from the track tossing it across the room, the mirror shatters against the wall and glass tinkles to the floor. There in the corner her beautiful daughters huddle together, Sarah sobbing as Emily rocks her in her arms. Their little faces streak with blood and black from their tears and the soot.

"Girls, we have to go, now!" she commands and the children look at her in surprise then leap at her. She carries her girls to the window of Sarah's room and uses the curtain to break out the glass.

"You have to jump and roll," she tells Emily and the helps her climb up on the sill. She watches as her daughter plummets the two stories to the ground and like the trooper she is, and she rolls as she hits the grass. Emily brushes her self off and stands, then holds her arms out to her.

"Come on!" she shouts.

Samantha turns to find Sarah staring at the door that is now engulfed in fire. The pink tiara wall paper around it blackens and flames race up the walls eating the little crowns as it grows.

"Sarah," Samantha says, "You need to jump."

"No," Sarah replies and continues to stare at the door.

"Sarah, now baby!" Samantha screams. "You have to jump!"

Samantha hauls her daughter to the window. Sarah is shaking and bloody tears fall down her face as she stares out the window at her sister. The fire is eating quickly through the pink-princess room and Samantha knows if they don't go now they won't get out at all

She picks her daughter up and clutches the girl to her chest, then leaps out the window. Her feet impact on the ground leaving a hole and she crouches low, her baby in her arms.

The sound of sirens roar in the distance and Sarah begins to wail with them.

"They're coming, mommy, they're coming!" she cries and Samantha grabs her girls by the hands and flees with them into the night.

They arrive at the safe house sometime close to dawn. Samantha can feel the pull of it at the back of her neck. They have run for hours to reach the house and she relaxes a little now. She steps up onto the porch and rings the doorbell desperately as she feels the first rays of light breech the horizon. The door opens and a very human woman stands at the entrance to their safe haven. A look of horror crosses the woman's face as she gasps and Samantha bares her fangs hissing at the woman. A man appears behind her as sunlight strikes the back of Samantha's exposed leg, heat sizzles and her flesh begins to smoke. Her girl's scream and huddle in front of their mom in her shadow that blocks the coming dawn.

"For Christ's sake," the man growls and yanks the little girls into the doorway shoving the human woman aside. Samantha lunges for the door through which her children have just disappeared and lands into a solid wall of muscle.

"Not you," he says as flames begin to eat her skin.

She hears her children sobbing for her from inside the house. She stares at the man confused and whispers, "Sanctuary."

"No," he replies and pushes her back into the light—she stumbles off the porch. "The children will be raised in the ways of our lord,'" he says and steps off the porch in front of her as her body smokes. The gold cross he wears around his neck glitters in the sunlight. "Back to hell with you demon," he shouts as he points his finger at her.

Samantha's body begins to burn with flames and she sees her brave Emily burst out the door, where the man catches her. He drags her back inside and the door slams. As her skin burns her last thoughts are of her daughters and she prays to their God for their safety.

Emily fights and strains against the hold of the human while Sarah sobs, bloody tears running down her face.

"You killed her!" Emily accuses and punches at the man's arms around her waist.

"Mother, get my bible!" shouts the man, "And the tranquilizers!"

Sarah watches in horror as her sister is held down and a long needle full of murky liquid is injected into Emily's arm. Emily stills and the man picks her up and lays her on the couch in the spotless living room. Her eyes round, she stands trembling afraid to move for what they may do to her.

When Emily wakes her head throbs and she shakes it to dislodge the blurriness in her eyes. Sarah sits nearby on the floor, sniffing gently and stroking the hair of a small doll. The scent of blood fills the room.

"They say we are to live here... " Sarah whispers while looking up at Emily.

Emily is angry. She has seen her father murdered and her brother is dead, too, she knows. And her mother—she watched as her mother burst into flames and the evil human did nothing.

"We're not staying here, Sarah," she says.

Emily rights herself on the couch next to the heavily muscled man. His head rolls to the side revealing a fresh wound. She feeds from the wound in the man's neck and then lets him slip off the couch onto the floor. Sarah, no longer crying, crouches over the woman near the front door. The small doll lies besides her seemingly staring wide-eyed as Sarah feeds. The seeds of darkness and hate have taken root and sprouted in the beautiful children.

"Let's go now," Emily says reaching for Sarah.

"Where will we go?" Sarah asks and climbs over the woman's

bloodless body and out the front door.

"It doesn't matter where," Emily says and embraces her sister. "As long as we're together we'll be okay."

They leave the house hand-in-hand. They pass the scorch mark on the ground that was once their beloved mother and Sarah pauses, anger burning in her chest. The darkness is thick in their souls and the ways of human monsters burnt deep into their memories.

The End

SO WEAK
By Gregory L. Hall

They know.

There's not much time left. I feel weaker by the minute. The hold on my sanity is rapidly slipping away. I am losing control of my very soul. And they know. I can tell by the look in their eyes. They know I'm not who I appear to be. And I'm changing into something horrible.

The pain. It will give them time to escape. It hits all at once and cripples me. The agony of the Changing is impossible to describe. Unless you're like me. It starts in my spine, a twisting and snapping of my vertebra. It shoots searing waves of flame into the base of my skull and down to my toes, burning me from the inside out. Then my shoulders break. Literally break as they slowly collapse and bend back with a violent yank. I can hear the bones crack like once mighty tree limbs caught in a hurricane. My legs buckle and unfold in a series of spastic jolts. I have to run while I can. For their safety and mine. Because once I change, I have no idea what I may do.

I find shadows deep in a back alley. The full moon. Why does it curse me so? I must hide and give into the change. Submit to the pain knowing it's the only way to stop it. As I feel my eyes blur over with thick cloudy puss, and my jaw bone shatters and reforms, one last thought echoes in what's left of my brain…where will I wake up this time?

The Blackness takes me.

***

I recall the taste of raw meat. How long have I been out? I have lost all track of time. I'm beginning to memorize the cycle.

Some are closer together. Some seem like I've been imprisoned forever. This seems to be one of the more torturous changes where I realize I can't wake up out of this nightmare. I'm trapped fully aware that my body and soul are not mine. I try to scream out but nothing can hear me in this hell. I don't exist. Not while the Monster owns me. All I can do is wait and hope that when I finally return to the world, all is right. I'm away from danger. I'll live to see another day. Live to correct everything my dark self has destroyed.

I let my mind swim in the mental fog but I can't even control inner thoughts that are rightfully mine. I receive mere flashes and try to fight and reach for more. Past the evil ones to those that anchor my sanity. Blood. Flesh. Meat torn from bone. Replaced by faces. The blank eyes that don't understand exactly how serious this danger is to them. To me. And then there are the smells. They flood my ability to concentrate. Such horrid and offensive smells that I can feel the vomit crawling back up my throat. The noises. So many conflicting, coming from every direction. I won't survive. But I have to. I have to.

The Monster is still in control. I try to see through its eyes but I'm afraid of what may be there. Can my brain handle it? Or will it break my already paper thin sanity into a billion scattered pieces to blow away in the dark winds.

I hold my breath in for a long moment. I must see what damage I have caused. I must get a clue as to where I am and where I will return when it is finally my turn to snatch my soul back from the hell this curse has strangled me with ever since that night. That brightly lit midnight when…

I see something. Through the opaque windows the Monster has allowed me. Standing before me yelling and screaming. Waving arms, throwing its weight forward and appearing to attack. Or at least threaten to. The word 'Bob' shoots into my mind. Bob? I'm lost but I won't give up. I try to cry out to Bob. Run, Bob. Run! What chance does Bob have?

Maybe a good chance. I feel so weak. Where is my strength? I can barely stand. I feel it in my knees. Off balance. I can't do this much longer. My breathing is so shallow. My heart beats as if my blood is meant to flow in trickles through my body. My yelling and screaming foe just might make it out of here alive. These legs. Arms. I can't do anything to hurt him. Run! Run while you can, Bob! I'm too weak. The Blackness is claiming me once again. I grasp memories while I can to ease my passage back into nothingness.

My home. I want to go home. I was so happy. You never realize how much freedom you have until it's stolen from you. There are those that complain about their lives but not me. I had the love of someone special to get me through tough times. The support of others to guide me. I had my brother...

He's dead. I remember now. The night the Monster attacked us. It was a careless walk in the woods. We had taken walks like this a thousand times before. Yes, I know. These woods were new to us. But both my brother and I were raised in the forests and no outdoor terrain was that foreign to us. Still, we should have known.

My brother saw it first. Wandering around in search of something. Hunting. Looking for a kill to devour. I wanted to leave but my brother stayed. Curiosity grabbed him and he had to see the Monster up close. It was just a stupid beast after all. My brother was far smarter and had trained his whole life to shadow animals in the wild. He was cocky whereas I saw the danger. I didn't get the chance to plead my case.

The Monster struck and my brother went down. I saw blood flying everywhere and heard my brother's screams for help. I froze. Again and again the Monster savagely attacked until the screaming stopped all together. Then it turned to me. I wasn't so quick. I don't know why I couldn't move. I only know I didn't. Our eyes met. Mine were alert, preparing for what may come next. Its eyes were vacant. No logic or reason. It lived to erase all living things in its path. The Monster split my skull. I retaliated.

Then the Blackness hit me like a falling redwood, hurling me into unconsciousness. I felt my soul rendered from my very core and the beast sucked me in. And for only an instant, I saw the world through its eyes. I knew what it knew. I discovered how such a creature could blindly ravage the living and walk away without need to repent. The Monster could do this because it had no soul. So it took mine.

I don't want to see through its eyes any longer. Bob's fate was not up to me now. And I don't want to think of home. I'll never know that home the same way again. I allow the Blackness to take me once again. Take me from the memories.

I miss my brother…

***

Pain! It jerks me from the unconscious hole in the depths of my brain. Where am I now? My scream escapes this time but it does nothing to ease the pain. It is more than any living creature should ever have to experience. Any creature is created to endure. The Changing. What evil entity chose this horror to reward a sinner? To punish a poor victim like me? Scream! I did nothing wrong! I don't deserve this pain! Stop ripping me apart!

Light. Breaking through. Yes! The light means hope has returned. The pain is tearing me in half but there is an ending! How long have I been trapped? I don't care. It doesn't matter now. The nightmare is ending! Bring me the pain!

My skeleton cracks and reshapes inside my flesh. The veil of darkness is swiftly dissipating. I see! The eyes that were not my own that I had to battle for mere glimpses into the outside world belong to me again. I feel the Monster losing control with each burst of scorching pain. Oh sweet wonderful pain! I embrace it now knowing it brings me my escape. Freedom from the Monster that steals my very being. I am me! I own my life, not the ugly beast that has no reason or purpose except for destruction! And when I snatch my life back, I will end this curse once and for all. The Monster will not return!

Help me! Give me the strength to see this transformation through! I need to reclaim myself! Please, before the pain explodes past the limits my fragile sanity can stand! Let me drop to the ground and know I am here again! Oh mother…Please! I can't do this anymore!

Sweat. I am drenched in sweat. Every part of my body soaked. My lungs. They burn as my chest heaves pulling in as much oxygen as I can hold. My ribs ache but I don't care. I need air. My nostrils rapidly convulse as the oxygen feeds my brain. Restores it. I can think again. I am here. I'm alive. Not the Monster. Me. I can feel my heart pounding as it pumps rivers of blood through my veins. My body sucks it in like nectar. The weakness melts away. I feel my strength returning.

Oh, my strength. I am powerful again. Fast. My precious stamina drenches the very fiber of my muscles and I feel fully recovered. The weakness of the Monster is gone. Legs that can barely launch a body forward. Limbs that struggle with the smallest amount of weight. Senses that do not work. Can you imagine the hell of relying on eyes that can not see? Ears that can not hear? A nose that couldn't detect prey if it was right in front of you? I do not know how the weak Monster within me survives but it will not get the chance to take me again. I own this body. This life.

I look about my surroundings. I am enclosed. Surrounded by wooden structures of varying sizes. Most like blocks. There is the humming and buzzing of man's harnessed energy. It fills the air. Air that smells rank and stale. Polluted with things not of nature. The smells are too many to describe but all offend me.

I've awakened here before. The Monster does most of his hunting here. Spends too much time here, prowling on the same grounds again and again. Stupid monster most certainly will get itself caught sooner than later. But I won't. I am much wiser. I know how to do this. I know how to feed.

I smell that I am not alone. My stealth is my pride and I silently glide behind another wooden block. There is a human here. A fleshy weak human like my Monster within. I know this scent. From the smallest of flashes my other self gives me a word. A simple word from its poor helpless mind trapped now where I have been for far too long. I do not know its meaning but I believe the word is for the human in the other room.

'Boss'.

I move through the darkness without a sound. I see everything. Every obstacle. My nose could lead me straight to my prey but there is no need. My eyes have already spotted it in the opening between enclosures. Oblivious. Fumbling around in lighting that is far too bright for any creature. No wonder these helpless humans spend half their existence squinting. Yet there it is piling objects into a thin box and talking loudly to someone who isn't there. It turns towards me and I see it with unblocked view now. I smile.

This is the human who threatens me. Attacks me. Yells and screams at me as if it actually believes it to be superior to me in some delusional way. Actually, my foe doesn't know about me. It knows my weaker Monster inside and abuses me through that shell. But it matters not. I am consumed with hunger. The need for raw meat. If this is the 'boss' that my Human Monster fears so much, let me take care of the matter once and for all.

My prey extinguishes the bright lights and exits its sanctuary. It finds more light, not as bright and moves clumsily into the long tunnel.

I need to say hello to Bob.

The End

Behind Walls
By Jezzy Wolfe

The paneling was such an eyesore.

THUNK!

"Goddamit!" Amelia dropped the offending hammer and promptly stuck her throbbing thumb into her mouth. In an attempt to hide the whitewashed obscenity, she hoped to cover the ugly expanse with pictures and rugs that she had found in the dusty attic of the recently restored Victorian. Every detail, every furnishing dated back to the turn of the century... except for that ridiculous paneling. Installed sometime in the late-70's, and then poorly disguised by several coats of white latex, the paneling screamed, "Tacky!"

"Sorry, Amy, but it still sticks out like a sore thumb." She turned and glared at Mark, still sucking on her injured digit, but it escaped his attention as he shook his head dejectedly. "I really don't think its thick enough to support all those nails you're driving into it."

"I just don't understand why they didn't yank out this crap when they did the repairs. I mean, they even took the time to replace the ceiling beams and the fireplace hearth. You'd think it would've been easy to rip this out and drywall it. I'm having a hard time locating the studs to nail into."

"Yeah," he agreed, "It was definitely an oversight. But you have been saving for years to buy this place, so maybe we can swing getting that wall replaced after we've settled in a bit." He glanced down, remembering the reason he'd interrupted her project. "Oh, almost forgot. I found this in one of your boxes. Thought you might want to hang it in here."

She gingerly handled the picture, faded and yellowed in its original frame, and smiled sadly. Taken just hours before her little brother Andrew disappeared, she never had the heart to replace the dilapidated frame and yellowed mats encasing the snapshot. It was just the two of them; she wore her favorite yellow sundress, and he was clad in ragged blue jeans and a green t-shirt. It was the day of their annual Fourth of July picnic in 1979. He had jumped on his bike to circle the block a few times that afternoon, and never returned.

Despite extensive search efforts, he was never found, and the case eventually went cold. But even as the family wallowed in grief, her mother refused to move, hoping that her son would find his way back home. She enlarged the snapshot and had it framed, hanging it above the fireplace so that no one would forget his face. Many countless cocktails of anti-depressants and alcohol later, her mother finally expired without ever seeing her little boy return.

Of course, after her mom's passing, they did move away. Not long after the vanishings started. Nearly a dozen children gone without a trace. They were never found, and the police never named any suspects. But that transpired years after Andrew's abduction, and her father simply decided they'd be better off somewhere else.

"I still don't understand why you'd want to come back here," Mark admitted. "What with your brother and the disappearances of the other children."

She gently hung the picture on a nail and stepped away. She felt closer to Andrew in that neighborhood, but she didn't want to come off morbid. Sighing heavily, she said, "I rode my bike past this place everyday, fantasizing about what it must be like to live in such a big old house. This is truly my dream come true." She shook herself from reverie and straightened her spine. "This wall, however," she gestured, "Is nothing but a nightmare."

"Eh. Nothing a glass of vino won't cure." He ruffled her hair and chuckled. "While I'm at it, I'll get you one, too."

"Oh, gee, thanks." She smirked over her shoulder as he

retreated, and turned back to glare at the wall once again. Three years ago, a small fire had gutted many of the rooms on the south end of the house, which prompted much needed renovations by the previous owners. But for some unknown reason they chose to leave the artificial walling, and simply painted it over to soften its appearance. Shortly after, the family relocated to the west coast, and the house stood unwanted on the market several years before she could snag it for herself. During the move-in she exceeded her tight budget, so she didn't have the funds to pull it out... not yet, anyway.

"Okay, you foul beast," she whispered dramatically. "Yield to the power of my interior design!" She brandished her hammer and squarely smacked a nail into the wood. As if taunting her, the wood bowed slightly and the nail bounced to the floor.

"I give up!" Amy cried petulantly, dropping the hammer and trudging to a worn couch. She flopped onto tattered cushions and was still sulking like a child when Mark brought her a glass of chilled chardonnay.

"You done already?"

"For now, yes. I'm too tired to fight with the atrocity anymore. Time to call it a night."

They finished their wine in a brief round of small talk, and settled down for the evening, weary from another day of unpacking. The comfort of clean sheets and a soft mattress quickly swept them both into much needed sleep.

In the still darkness her eyes shot open. Momentarily disoriented, she thought perhaps she was still dreaming, but the soft whirs and vaguely visible movement of the ceiling fan indicated otherwise. She lay very still, waiting for her pounding heart to slow, unsure what had disturbed her sleep.

But then she heard it. The soft scratches that seemed to come from under her bed. Barely discernable, yet they reverberated loudly in her ears. She shuddered and held very still, until it came again. Five tiny scrapes across the floorboards, almost like tiny footsteps.

She relaxed and drifted back into her coma of sleep. *Just mice,* she consoled herself. *I'll call the exterminator tomorrow.*

A couple cups of coffee worked wonders. She barreled through the morning tirelessly, unpacking clothes, dishes, and small boxes of knick knacks. Mark unloaded furniture from the moving truck and situated them in the rooms she designated. It was after lunch before Amy remembered the midnight interruption.

"I'm gonna call my father's old exterminator, if he's still in business. Better to have the house treated now before we unpack everything." She thumbed through yellow pages, fingers sliding over columns of numbers until she spotted the familiar ad. "Wow! He's still around. I wonder if he'll remember me."

An elderly man answered her call. "Bristow speaking."

"Mr. Bristow, hi. My name is Amy Platt. You used to treat my father's house, over on Maple Court. Reggie Platt?" By his silence, she realized he'd forgotten. She was embarrassed she had mentioned it.

"Oh, yes. I remember. The ranch with the blue shutters." He had a surprisingly good memory. "You're little Amy."

"Well, I'm not so little anymore," she laughed. "I was wondering if you could come take a look at my house. I think we have mice."

"You still there, are you? Been a long time since I looked at it. You're probably due for a visit. It's 5109 Maple Street, right? I'd be happy to drop by."

"No sir. I just moved into the Lancaster house. Over on Old Oak Drive?"

He went quiet again. She waited patiently, figuring he was trying to remember the house she indicated. He coughed a few times and cleared his throat.

"Oh yes." Awkwardly, he maundered, "Actually, I retired a few years back. Arthritis, you know. Worst case my doctor ever seen, he said."

She was confused. "I thought you said you'd be happy to drop by?"

"I can't go crawling around anymore. Too much on my knees, unfortunately. But you can call Bob Smith. He's real good, and he could probably get there quickly."

"Yes, please. That would be great. What's his number?" She jotted the name and number on a scrap paper and mumbled her thanks.

Mark watched with curiosity from the kitchen table. "What was that all about?"

"I have no idea. He seemed ready to come by, until I gave him the address." She puzzled over his strange reaction as she dialed Bob Smith's number. Fortunately, the younger man was eager to do business, and agreed to be there in an hour. Bristow's unusual behavior still baffled her, but she dismissed it as nothing more than elderly quirkiness.

She was waiting by the door when Mr. Smith arrived, flashlight and clipboard in hand. Amy promptly led him to the bedroom, describing the noises she heard the night before.

"Certainly sounds like mice to me," he agreed. "I'll take a look around; maybe crawl up under the house. If you got mice, there will be droppings lying about. I can either lay traps or leave poison, whichever you prefer."

"Whatever you think is best is fine with us. I'm just glad you came out so quickly. I want to finish unpacking."

"Yes, ma'am. I'll get started on it." He had turned on his flashlight and was inspecting the baseboards when she left the room.

They were sitting in the kitchen when he re-joined them. "I didn't see any droppings or mouse holes anywhere. I'm gonna go check underneath, now. There may be some spaces down there they can climb through."

"Would you care for a drink first?" Amy offered politely.

"That would be great, if it's not too much trouble."

Mark offered him a seat at the table. "Have you been in business long?"

"Naw. Just moved here about three years ago. I like it; it's a nice area. Much quieter than Jersey."

"It must really boost your business, getting all those referrals from Mr. Bristow."

"Bristow referred you? That's a first," he replied, draining his glass of iced tea. "That man is my biggest competitor. He's a tenacious old coot!"

Mark and Amy shot suspicious glances at each other as he stood. "I'll go see if I can find anything crawlin around down there."

"Thanks," she murmured.

"Bristow must have momentary arthritis," Mark suggested lamely.

After another half hour, Bob resurfaced. He was out of breath, panting erratically as he fiddled with his clipboard. "I didn't find anything, Ms. Platt. Are you sure what you heard wasn't the house settling?"

"I'm positive," she declared indignantly.

There was a strange look on his face, and not only was he flushed and sweaty, he had also paled several shades. "Thanks for the tea. I won't charge you for the house call." He hurried towards the front door, with Amy on his heels.

"Wait, Mr. Smith! Did you find anything at all? Structural damage? Maybe it's termites."

"The wood has been replaced recently. I didn't find evidence of pests. Of any sort." He smiled weakly. "I'm sorry, but I'm running late for my next appointment. Ya'll have a good afternoon."

He jumped into his truck and tore out of the driveway like a bat out of hell. Amy watched on through a cloud of dust and gravel, shaking her head in bewilderment. "I don't understand. Why did he leave so fast? He was here for over an hour; he should have billed us for the house call, regardless."

"One less thing to pay," Mark shrugged. "At least we don't have mice. That's always good news."

"If it's not mice, it's definitely something else." She noted his skeptical stare and bristled. "I know what I heard, Mark."

"Sweetie, you woke up in the middle of the night after a long hard day of work. Your mind could've easily been playing tricks on you. Forget about it. We got other things to worry about, anyway." He led her back to the kitchen. "Like, for instance, what you're gonna make me for dinner?"

She swatted him and laughed half heartedly. Leave it to Mark to think with his belly.

After finishing for the day, they opted for fast food. She was too tired to cook and wash dishes. An hour after relaxing in front of the television, they decided to retire for the night. Amy soundly put the events of the afternoon behind her. She probably imagined the noises. It wouldn't be the first time her imagination ran away with her. She slid between the sheets and was asleep almost immediately.

The scraping jarred her from another pleasant dream. The scratches were longer and louder than the night before. *No pests my ass*, she thought bitterly. Carefully, she climbed out of bed, trying not to rouse Mark, who was snoring softly. A flashlight stood sentinel on the end of a bureau. She knelt on the floor beside the bed and flipped on the beam.

Unless the dust bunnies had started to make noises, there was nothing visible to account for what she heard. Settling on all fours, she held her breath, waiting for more sounds. She didn't have to wait long.

It came from behind the baseboard. Six distinctive scratches, like a rake across the wall's backside. Smith claimed he found no mouse holes or droppings, but something had gotten in there. If it wasn't a mouse, then it had to be some other furry pest. Possibly a squirrel. At least she knew whatever it was wouldn't be crawling into bed with them. She went back to bed with the intention of searching for herself the next day.

They pillaged through the day like soldiers on a mission. The last of the furniture and boxes were moved off the truck, and she'd organized the kitchen and bathrooms accordingly. Early into the afternoon, Mark decided to turn the truck back in to the rental office since it was no longer needed. As it happened, there were several boxes that needed to be carried to the attic.

"I was planning on going up there, anyway," she said as he walked out the door. "I'll carry them up."

"What are you, crazy? Those boxes weigh a ton. Wait till I get back, and we'll both go up. Besides, if you think a squirrel has gotten in, I doubt you'll want to wrestle it out alone."

She had to admit, it made sense. She had no desire to tango with a pissed squirrel. "All right, then. I guess I'll go back to the paneling."

He chuckled. "Now that I don't mind missing out on. You have fun with it."

He winked as she stuck out her tongue at him. But as he drove away, her spirits sank. She busied herself with many other small chores so she could avoid the dismal task of concealing the wall. But there was no point in putting it off any longer. She would grit her teeth and do what she could, and in another couple months she would hire a small team to remove every bit of that tasteless paneling out and replace it with a real wall.

She caught herself at the threshold, a curious thought striking her. Why was she so reluctant to deal with the wall? It was just a wall, after all, and a temporary one at that. But she avoided the room like a repellant magnet. Usually, she didn't even glance inside as she passed by.

Past the den, a short hallway bent to the left leading to their bedroom, an office, and the master bathroom. In fact, the bedroom was directly behind the den, but she didn't have weird sensations in there.

Weird sensations. That was it, exactly. It was more than the wall; it was the uneasiness that cloaked her whenever she was in there. Her edginess simply focused on the wall because it was so out of place. Haunted paneling? She scolded herself for being so silly, and marched resolutely into the room, this time without hesitation. Whatever the problem, it was time to put it aside permanently.

A large ornate mirror was propped by the doorway, waiting to be mounted in place. She had a hard time putting up the hooks on which to hang it, but she decided it would be the first task she'd conquer. Looking over the supplies she'd left out for the job, she realized the nails were far too small. Easy enough to correct. A scavenge through her tool box yielded larger nails. She tucked one between her lips and began her decorative attack.

Retrieving the hammer from the floor, she positioned the nail against a strip of panel resting over a stud, and laid a direct hit on its head. It sunk deep, accompanied by a splintering crack. "Oh, that's just great!"

A two inch rent jutted vertically from the nail, running along what appeared to be a fissure in one of the panel grooves. Just rewards for not drilling a starter hole first. She frowned, fingering the split, and tugged on the nail. She wouldn't be able to hang anything on fractured wood.

But as she pulled, the seam split further, extending all the way to the floor, and back up towards the ceiling. She wouldn't be able to wait a couple months for the renovation; it would have to be done immediately. She inched her hand into the crack and pulled the edge towards her. To her surprise, the paneling swung outwards.

She found a door.

Frozen in shock, she gazed into the yawning blackness. For a narrow space between walls, it seemed quite... cavernous. Ordinarily it would make the most sense to close the door and nail it shut, but her instincts screamed otherwise. She dashed to her bedroom and grabbed the flashlight, and hurried back to the opening.

The hole absorbed light like a sponge, so she projected the beam straight into the doorway. Veils of dust-laced cobwebs danced before her, but past the filmy gauze she could make out the opposite barrier. A gap of 3 feet lay between the paneling and her bedroom. She cringed at the idea of what may be crawling around in the dark gap, but her inquisitiveness was overwhelming. Cautiously, she brushed the webs aside and stepped into the space.

It smelled of the musk of old wood and paper, tinged with mildew. Nothing abnormal. She swung the beam of the flashlight in either direction, but it was too dark to see where the space ended. If she didn't know better, she'd swear it was a tunnel. But to where? Maybe she'd find stairs to the second floor or the attic. Better yet, what if she found a secret room? Her imagination was running away with possibilities. Buoyed by a sense of adventure, she turned to the left and felt her way along the wall.

Eventually, she saw the end of the passage. She focused the light straight ahead, shuffling slowly as her free hand gripped exposed beams. She was almost two feet from the far end when the floor disappeared.

With a startled squeal she stepped back, the music of raining pebbles announcing the pit's presence. Leaning over, she cast the beam into the abyss. Determining the depth of the hole was impossible from her perch. The floor had collapsed, the boards most likely decayed with rot and termite infestation. She was sick with growing dread. If the wood started giving way here, it would eventually compromise the stability of the surrounding structure.

She squinted into the gloom, attempting to identify the massive rubble heaped beneath the opening. Looked more like sticks than floorboards, but there was so much dirt caking the mound that she couldn't see the mass clearly. The house was in worse shape than she thought. She groaned at the thought of extensive repairs, and scuffled back towards the den.

A squirrel could've gotten between the walls through that hole, she thought. That's where the scratching came from. The knowledge was somewhat comforting, more so than the possibility of a furry infestation. But the rationale didn't uproot the nagging awareness in her gut.

She continued past the opening to the den and navigated the unexplored passageway, watching closely for more structural collapses. Focusing along the bottom of the walkway, she looked for signs of a vigilante squirrel. After only thirty seconds or so, the tunnel abruptly ended. If she guessed correctly, she was right behind her bed.

She stood in front of a makeshift wall, boards nailed over each other haphazardly, rocks and bricks shoved into the open spaces between the timbers. A professional wasn't responsible for such shoddy construction. Quite possibly the framework was crumbling, and the havoc was an amateur attempt to support the inner walls. Shrugging, she removed the stones easily, unpleasantly calculating the extensive costs of her money pit. Her sinking spirit was a distraction from the growing warning bells ringing in her head.

The rocks piled at her feet, dislodging a shower of dust and dirt, wringing more than a few sneezes as she continued deconstructing the barrier. The wood, dry rotted and splintering, groaned loudly as she pulled each board free, but offered little resistance against her determined efforts. Once completely discarded around her, she illuminated the hole left behind the ragged wall.

The smell struck her first; a pungent smell of decay and rot, of many years passed in the dank darkness. She frowned, peering closer at strange gray shapes that interrupted the glare of her visual accessory. Slowly, the truth of what was hiding behind the walls of her home assaulted her. But it was the tattered dirty green and faded, frayed denim that finally pushed her into the black of unconsciousness.

Police and investigators were scouring the premises when Mark returned home, via taxi. Amy didn't answer the phone when he called for a ride, and he had grown concerned. His apprehension wasn't relieved by the yellow crime scene tape marking off the property, either. He found Amy shakily sipping on a hot mug of coffee as she whimpered responses to an inquiring officer's questions. It was a good half hour before he could make sense of what had happened.

Ironically, the family that purchased the house from Freeman Lancaster's estate never reported any alarming findings during their renovations. And although the fire hadn't damaged that side of the house, the repairs were made throughout. In the basement, an ill-placed brick barrier boxed the burial mound, but no one had questioned its unnecessary presence. Even though it was suspicious they chose to leave intact the paneling with its secret door as they restored the rest of the house, they weren't to blame for the heinous crime. They lived in the old Victorian fifteen years before putting it on the market. The bones, however, were more than twenty-one years old.

Investigators turned the house inside out looking for more remains. An old trunk shoved into a back corner of the walled-off bone pit held the remnants of three children. The bones of nine others had been dumped unceremoniously into the hole- most likely after that area had been closed off. Andrew had been the first of thirteen, and the only one with a tomb of his own.

The dismal closet was no longer his coffin. Two weeks later, a beautiful cherry box was laid in the ground beside their mother's grave.

After 28 years, Andrew had finally come home.

THE END

Demise
By Alexzan Burton

The voices

So close, I can feel them.
Like they are right behind me.

Paranoid.

Turn to face them and no one is there.
But I hear them.

They are telling me to hurt you.

I'm sorry.
I hate to do this, you know I love you
But the voices.
They are so persistent and they won't let me go.

I have to be free...

You scream.

Shhh.
Please don't, that hurts me.
I don't want to hear you cry.
Don't be afraid.
It will only hurt for a while.

The voices, shrill and agonizing.
They are piercing my brain.

There is no time for begging,
Don't make this harder
Than it has been

Don't look at me that way,
It hurts me inside.
You know I don't want to do this
But I am not the one to decide.

They tell me to start with the knife.
They want me to cut you.

I am so sorry...
Please don't cry like that.

I have to make a nice long cut from your bellybutton
To your throat.
It won't last long
It won't even hurt.

Please! Don't scream!
You are making the voices
Yell at me more.

I told them it wasn't my fault,
I cannot stop you.
But they said that I can...

'The needle', they said.
Sew her lips shut.

Don't fight me,
I am just doing what they tell me
To do.
Can't you understand?

If I don't do this, they will kill me.
Do you want them to kill me?

Now, hold still.
Don't jerk like that,
You will rip your lips open.

It's just 12 little holes
So I can run the strings through.
Just a few little X's
Should do.

Now, you are silent,
But still those tears.

How it hurts me so...
But the voices,
They won't let me go.

A slash through your arm,
And the voices cease
Just a bit.

Remember, I love you.
I would never hurt you
If I had my own way.

Now is the time.
The voices say you must die.
Please close your eyes...
I don't want yours to meet mine.

The voices
No longer ceased,
They are screaming and taunting.
They want this to end..
Oh, your screams are so haunting.

I plunge the knife
Deep into your chest.
Your sewn shut lips
Tear from the stress.

Your screams are all
That I can hear
And when those cease,
There is no one near.

The voices have left me
Alone with this mess.
There's no one to save me...
Nothing is left.

What have I done,
My friend?
Your turtured body

Is now my deceit.

The voices betray me,
I beg at your feet.
Redeem me.

I look down at myself,
I see I am covered in blood.
My body is weakened and
I now give up...

The blood is my own..
The voices were my suicide.
And now it is over...
I am my own demise.

Voices In The Dark
by Buffy Vincent

"That bastard," she thought as she heard his laughing voice boom down the hallway. She could see him in her mind's eye touching the *whore's* lithe little body, running his fingers up her pale porcelain throat, brushing across her blood red lips. If Cadence could scream in outrage she would. If she could move she'd kill them both delivering slow and torturous deaths. Her mind seethed as that bastard shot her images of his tryst with the little whore. She saw bare flesh against bare flesh, fangs scraping along throbbing veins. Cadence squeezed her eyes shut and mentally built a wall to keep him out. It was all she could do. Her fists clenched and unclenched at her sides as she pictured the wall while he pushed at it from the outside. She heard the asshole laugh again and the whore giggled in delight. She ground her teeth and fought for emotional control.

How had this happened? How had she gotten herself into this? That stupid little whore would be next—she'd be in Cadence's place. For a second she wondered who had come before the whore, then realized it didn't really matter. They would get theirs. When the time was right she would be free, even if she had to wait a century to exact revenge on the bastard. And, of course, the little whore would be dead. He never kept the children for long.

Cadence's mind began to drift as blood loss began to effect her. As her mental wall began to weaken, the bastard threw images at her. It was like watching a speed metal video she wished could be shut off. She ignored it instead concentrating on singing Rob Zombie's Dragula. She passed out.

Pain shot through her shoulder moving down her arm. It

forced her wide awake. It was pitch black when her eyes opened. Cadence tried to move to get to her burning shoulder when her stomach cramped. Hunger pains seized her insides and she moaned.

Cadence

She moaned again at the sound of her name and tried to shift. More stomach pain, more pain in her shoulders at the action.

Cadence? Are you hungry baby?

Images of blood washed her mind. A knife sliced across a pale wrist. She clenched her jaw which caused her teeth to ache as she anticipated the coming blood. Crimson welled up. A thin line of red trickled down the wrist. Pain engulfed her again and she thought, "Fuck you, Derrik," with as much mental force as possible hoping her thoughts literally screamed in his head. Cadence heard the bastard's muffled laughter again and the image faded. God she hurt! Just a sip of the whore's blood would alleviate her pain a little. She tried to tug her shoulder free but new pain blazed through her and the smell of blood assaulted her nostrils as her shoulder tore afresh. Blood wormed its way down her left arm, then tickled her finger tips, finally dripping down her thigh. She felt the whole progress of that line of blood, until she thought she'd go mad. It was like Chinese water torture. She could feel it, smell it, but she couldn't touch it. She longed to taste it in her mouth, feel it wash over parched lips and cool her throat. Cadence sighed. How long had she been here? It couldn't have been that long, because the wounds were still fresh. He really was a bastard to do this to her. Why not just kill her and get it over with? She was in the house still, but where?

She tried to call out.

"Hello?" her voice squeaked. She tried louder, but her vocal cords wouldn't cooperate. Cadence tipped her head back raising her chin a little. That's when she felt the pain in her throat. The skin ached and she could feel it trying to knit shut. It tingled like it always did when it repaired itself.

What had the bastard done to her? Why couldn't she

remember? Cadence began trying to retrace her steps in her mind.

Cadence had come home a little over a month ago and discovered Derrick in bed with the whore. She heard the sounds long before reaching the bedroom door. Throwing the keys on the hall table, she went directly for the bedroom. The door bounced off the wall.

"Hi honey, I didn't know you'd be home yet," he said rising from the blonde's throat, his mouth covered in blood. The room wreaked of it…that and sex. Several puncture wounds dotted the blonde's throat and breasts. She wondered where else tiny puncture marks probably penetrated her flesh, places that couldn't be seen.

"Stop it, Derrik, you're going to kill her," Cadence said moving forward into the room. She saw the blonde had gone pale-white, her eyes glossy and staring far off. "Damn it, Derrik, she's already dead!" she snapped and grabbed for the pale wrist.

"She not dead…not yet," he chuckled. "I needed a new toy, Cay," Derrik said as if for some reason that made it okay.

"You promised, Derrik! You promised this wouldn't happen any more, that you could be faithful and feed outside the house," she said dropping the wrist. She put both hands on her hips.

"Did I say that? Darling, I think you're mistaken," he replied and licked the slow trail of blood off the whore's neck.

"I'm leaving and when I get back that…that… whore better be gone. And for God's sake change the damn sheets!" She spun away and stormed toward the door. "I have to sleep here too!" she barked over her shoulder storming out of the room.

"CADENCE!"
The scream came loud and clear startling her, and she jolted her wounded shoulder. Flesh tore around her shoulder again with the motion. Groggy, her head rolled against the wall. It was the whore.

Every time she drifted off the whore screamed again and brought her back. Cadence was really going to enjoy killing her.

"You're in there…I'm out here…and you're not getting out," the whore sang while laughing through the wall.

She heard the stupid girly giggle echo down the hall. What she would give to have the obnoxious brat in front of her. Somewhere a door slammed and the whore squealed with delight. The bastard was home again.

"Look what I brought home, darling," he said in a rich velvet voice that now made Cadence's skin crawl with hatred. Having superior hearing, Cadence knew this was going to be a long night.

"Oh Derrik!" the whore said. "He's lovely. Look at all that brown hair. Can I control him?"

Cadence wanted to laugh. Derrik would never allow it, not in a million years—he was a control freak. It totally surprised her when he replied, "Sure! Anything for you, baby." She rolled her eyes at the sugary tone, then laughed when the boy—and it was a boy not a man—came out from under the influence of Derrik's mind control. The boy began yelling in fright.

"Where am I?" he cried in a desperate voice. "Who the hell are you?"

The whore whispered something and the boy became silent again.

"Look!" she squealed again. "I did it!" The sound of clapping accompanied her words. Surely Derrik hadn't turned her—a mere child. Cadence sent her mind out in search and was surprised to feel two humans in the outer room. He was playing with the whore, making her believe she was a vampire.

"Here let me undress him," Derrik said.

Cadence could just imagine him taking each piece of clothes off the boy. He was most likely a young adult like the whore. Derrik liked them young, thin and little more than children. She drifted into a dream of when they had first met.

Cadence had just turned 18 and had been jazzed about her new life in the big city. She had literally bumped into him on the street.

"Oh, sorry!" she told him dropping the grocery bag she held.

"Oh no…it was me. Here, let me help you with that." His hand touched hers and heat shot directly to her groin. If she had only known then, hadn't been so stupid… If, if, if! She twitched in her sleep remembering.

Derrik's long blond hair was pulled back in a pony-tail and his cashmere coat brushed the ground as he bent to help retrieve the groceries.

"That's the last of it," he said as his eyes found hers.

Cadence forgot how to breathe and, for a minute, nearly choked as she stared into those sky blue depths.

"T-Thank you," she stuttered.

"I know this forward, but can I buy you a coffee?" he asked with a grin.

"I'd love a coffee," she responded.

That night she never made it home. The coffee and flirting had reared its head and before she knew it, she was pressed up against his apartment door, head spinning from his ravishing kisses. Derrik broke free long enough for her to moan as he trailed down her neck. Cadence's common sense left her that night and she soon found herself being tossed on a bed, her clothes torn from her body. She never thought to protest as he slid between her thighs and her body clenched in anticipation. His finger rubbed her swollen clit, readying her. She cried out and arched, offering to his ministrations. Before she had time to feel pain he thrust inside and stole her virginity. She remembered the feel of him inside of her, how she felt stretched and so full it almost hurt. She instinctively wrapped her legs around his waists as he took her. His tongue ran over her skin and she grabbed his head, fingers tangling in the soft gold hair. She moaned as he bit into her pulse. At the first pulling of her blood, fire ripped through her body. She arched again gushing around him.

"CADENCE!"

She woke to the whore's voice again. This time it was a scream of pleasure.

"Oh! Derrik you feel so good!" the girl's muffled moan said.

Cadence gagged at the thought even though she had just been dreaming of Derrik. How strange that love could turn to hate so quickly! Her body now screamed in pain while standing there, head against the wall, sight blinded by lack of light. It felt like her stomach was on fire as it clenched and roared with hunger's pain. The moans of the whore assaulted her ears, and the whore's screams of pleasure became quite painful in the dark. She blinked and listened to them. Derrik groaned and Cadence's teeth slid out. Even her body knew that blood would come with his climax.

I hate him, she thought. Something scratched at her bare feet then bit her big toe. She winced and let curse words fly, calling Derrik every demeaning name she could think of. Her stomach clenched and her teeth hurt, as she smelled her own blood again. God, she couldn't win for losing!

Cadence thought about how long it had been before he changed her—three months? Four? He had at least waited until she had fully developed a womanly shape otherwise she'd have been trapped in a premature body undeveloped throughout eternity. She settled into the memory ignoring her body's request for blood.

"Hey, baby, I'd like you to meet Jaime—isn't she cute?" he said as though this was a first time occurrence.

"No, Derrik!" Somewhere she had finally found a backbone and began telling him *no*.

"Oh, come on, Cay," he whined, "Look at her pretty neck."

"Does she even know she's been taken? Or did you just put her under before she even met you?" she sneered.

"Does it matter? She's so pretty. You like redheads...I know you do," he purred and ran his fingers through the long curls.

"Yes, damn it! It matters. I don't understand any of this...or you any more!" Cadence was yelling at him now. "I don't want a puppet to play with. It's sick! Besides, how old is Jaime, Derrik? She doesn't even look 18!"

Derrik began to pull the shirt from the young woman's body and he licked her neck tauntingly.

"Come on, Cay. I promise you'll like it. It'll be like before you turned."

"Before *you* turned me, I couldn't even object, you dick!" She balked saying, "I'm not doing this any more...I have a choice."

He moved so fast she was pinned against the wall in a heartbeat and that's when things went from bad to worse.

"Do this or you'll be sorry, darling. I am your sire and don't think that doesn't mean I won't take you out if I need to. You were turned because you understood," he hissed between clenched teeth. "Don't let me down now...don't make me kill you."

She turned blue as he held her by the throat to the wall. Her first thought was to run fast and as far.

"You run and I'll hunt you down," he spat. "Just try it. You wouldn't be the first." He licked his own spit off the side of her face. "Now," he said putting her on her feet, "if you'd be so kind as to take Jaime to the bedroom...I'll be right there."

Just like that Cadence had lost.

She spent weeks trying to learn to build a wall to keep him out of her head, but she hadn't tried to leave. Every week he brought home someone else and she sinned right along with him, using them like puppets, taking pleasure and blood from their young innocent bodies.

Until the whore that is.

"Baby you awake?" The words were followed by sounds: thud, thud, thud! The noise roused her to full alertness. Derrik's voice was muffled, but she could hear it plain as day. The voices in the dark always persisted, waking her from slumber to her personal hell in inky blackness.

"You brought this on yourself," he said. "I told you to leave her alone."

"Let," she croaked against her throat's protests, "Let me out."

"Not yet, Cay. You haven't learned your lesson yet."

The sound of his footfalls trailed away.

What had she done? She couldn't remember. Her stomach was a constant knot of pain now, the hunger gnawing, her head swimming with thoughts as she tried to keep her eyes open. She moved her hand when her nose began to itch and her shoulder throbbed again. Forcing away the pain, she inched that hand forward until she could feel the wall with her fingertips. She crawled her hand up the wall in front of her, her fingers acting like spider legs, and she felt the brush of her breasts. She turned her hand wincing again and followed it over her chest and up toward her shoulder. There protruding from the left shoulder was a cold piece of metal. She wrapped her fingers around it. Groaning, she tried to pull it free. Pain ripped through her and her shoulder throbbed, right before the warm trickle ran down her torso. The scent of her fresh blood brought out her teeth again. Cadence began to laugh a low croak of a sound and the shoulder shook, causing the skin and muscle around the spike to burn and throb, but she couldn't help it. She laughed harder and louder.

"What's that?" the whore asked.

"I don't know…" the bastard answered.

His quiet steps came closer to the prison. She laughed at the pain, at him and cursed him mentally; loud enough that she knew he could hear. It was her against the voices in the dark, for that had been what her world had been reduced to: pain and voices in darkness.

"It's her, isn't it?" the whore gasped. "What if she gets out?"

"Don't worry, she won't get out…" Derrik's voice trailed of as if unsure and Cadence laughed harder, her throat gasping at the pain in her whole body.

When the fit stopped she grabbed the spike again with renewed vigor.

"Lock me up…bastard," she grumbled and pulled against the spike. It didn't move but she wouldn't give up, not this time. "Bastard!" she tried to shout, but it came out a growl. Wrapping her fingers around the metal she pushed back and forth, back and forth. She had nothing better to do and all the time in the world.

She should have killed the little whore when she'd had the chance.

Cadence drank down one last gulp of rich coppery wetness. Then she licked the twin wounds and pushed away from the girl. She felt cheap and stupid above all else. How had it come this far? Had she sunk so low as to feed on this woman child? The little blonde sighed, sated as Derrik pulled out of her then grabbed Cadence's mouth to his.

"Mmmmm," he moaned, "I love the taste of blood in your mouth."

Cadence cringed at those words. She hated this, all of it. It made her skin crawl. Every time it had been the same, different people every week…until this one. The blonde whore. She hated the way the whore looked at Derrik and the way he looked at her, the hunger and lust in his eyes when he saw her naked. She was always naked when he was home. Cadence pulled away and broke the kiss. The whore stared at them with a pouty look, as if to say *what about me?* Derrik reached down and pulled the whore up between them. Cadence shifted away and watched as his large arms engulfed the tiny body. The whore kissed him, and Cadence watched as her tongue slipped sloppily in and out of his mouth.

"I love you, Derrik," the blonde cooed and rested her head on his chest as he stroked her hair.

"I love you too, baby," he replied lovingly.

Cadence had to leave the bed before she puked on both of them. How many times had he said that to her? And, like an idiot, she had believed it. He left the whore on the bed and followed Cadence to the bathroom where she turned on the shower. She had to get clean to wash the grime and sin off her skin. She pretended like he wasn't there and stepped into the shower. She sighed heavily when she realized he trailed after her.

"What's wrong?" he had actually had the nerve to ask.

She laughed before thinking better of it. It caused him to hiss in warning, like a damn cat.

"I just don't like her," she said then stuck her head under the faucet to drown herself.

He grabbed her by the shoulders and jerked her out of the spray.

"Learn to like her…she's not going anywhere," he said and bent to her throat.

She pulled away, turning from him, but he held tight and it was like he was raping her. Derrik sank his teeth into her vein. Treacherous heat shot into her groin and she moaned in spite of herself. By this time she didn't know if she really wanted this on some level or if he had conditioned her to like it. After a few drinks he pulled back and kissed her hard on the mouth.

"I love you," he purred as if he had proven a point.

She turned into the spray to wash off the saliva and the taint of another night spent with him.

Quiet had fallen over the house when next Cadence's eyes opened. Her left hand still dangled uselessly at her side, but the right was already in motion toward the spike. She inhaled sharply as the movement made things that shouldn't hurt scream in protest. She began wiggling the spike again, back and forth, excited when she thought it moved. Pushing against it harder, she heard a creak behind her. She was making progress.

While wiggling the metal she began to call to the whore through her mind. She was a vampire after all. Shouldn't she use those powers to help herself?

Come to me, she breathed and sent the compulsion to the whore. *Come to me...I need you.*

Cadence heard the girl's feet shuffle in the hall toward her prison, slow and languid footfalls. Cadence felt her heart beat pulsing down the hall, and if she strained hard enough she could actually hear it's steady rhythm. The promise of blood made her growl.

Then Derrik called out to the whore and Cadence dropped her control.

"Come back to bed," he said and the steps quickly retreated away down the hall.

She could use this, she thought, pulling against the resistant metal. Cadence could use the whore. She was still human and Cadence knew how to control humans. All she had to do now was wait until the bastard left the house.

And wait she did, standing in the dark, legs cramping from her weight and ears aching at the empty silence. Every once in a while she felt a mouse scurry across her toes and smelled the gamey scent of blood as it rushed past. If she could only reach one, maybe the pain from not feeding would stop. She tried in vain to lean to the right and stretch out her fingers to catch one. With her shoulder pinned she couldn't quiet reach. Not to mention the space didn't allow her to bend at the knees. What she wouldn't give to be able to bend her knees! Her neck was tight with tension as she stood in the small space, the wall at her back. If she didn't know better she would swear the space was getting smaller, closing in on her. Cadence closed her eyes and counted her breaths to try and pass the time. The dark engulfed her even behind her eyelids and she wanted to scream to break the silence. If only she could.

Dreams of blood filled her head. She was bathing in a river of blood, while green grass grew on the banks. She drank greedily cupping her hands to her mouth and let it slide down her throat. Such beautiful dreams, she felt like her very pores were absorbing the crimson river. When she stood the blood drooled from her body and pooled in the grass as she left the feast. Then the dream shifted.

She was in bed with Derrik holding her down and the whore between her legs. She tried to fight but he was overpowering her. Somehow she managed to get a foot between the girl and her body and pushed the whore off the bed. The girl hit the floor with a thud and the scent of blood filled the air. Derrik released her and ran to the whore.

"You could have killed her!" he screamed from the floor as he cradled the whore's head in his lap.

Cadence didn't respond. Instead, she merely closed her legs and pulled them under her. She glared at Derrik and wanted to tell him to go to hell. She wasn't his puppet any more. She wouldn't let him force his whore on her any longer.

He stood and brought her back to the bed, gently laying the fragile body on the crimson stained sheets. "Get out," he snarled at Cadence.

She just stared at him unable to move as he glared at her.

"Get OUT!" he shouted and the windows rattled.

She scrambled off the bed and ran from the room. She was shaking as she pulled on her clothes and moved towards the door to leave the house. She felt him behind her as her hand reached for the handle. His eyes burned holes into the back of her head.

"Don't go," he whispered and she stopped dead in her tracks.

She thought about turning the knob and just walking out of his life. It's what she should have done, run while she had the opportunity. Somewhere inside a little voice whispered *no*. A very scared little voice that somehow started to make sense the longer she hesitated, until finally fear washed over her and she turned around.

"Come back to bed," he said and like the naive little child she still was inside, she did just that. She walked to him shedding her clothes, until she stood in front of him, nude and stripped bare to her soul. Cadence let him into her mind and then stepped into his arms as he opened them. She began to sob as he held her.

"It's alright, baby, you'll always be my little girl," Derrik told her stroking her hair. She wanted to believe him so badly. She wanted him to love her, but how could he? She wasn't like the ones he chose, young or frail, nor was she even dependent upon him any more. She could take care of herself. Cadence shook in his arms as those fears manifested in her mind. He had already replaced her...replaced her with the whore who would boldly do anything without question. Cadence followed him willingly to the bed and climbed in bedside *her.* She slipped to sleep in his arms. Had she been together at all she would have known that he was in her mind controlling her again.

The front door banged and startled her awake.

"I don't know why he's so mad," the whore grumbled passing by. That caught Cadence's attention. He had left. Left *her* alone. Now was her chance...it had to be now. She pulled herself together and focused. Then she called to the whore.

Come to me, I need you.

She heard the footfalls stop at the end of the hall and the slowly shuffle back towards her.

That's it, come find me...I need your help, she compelled.

The steps stopped outside of the wall and a small thud came through. Please, please let her know how to open it, she prayed. Gentle thuds then scraping as Cadence urged her on.

Yes, that's it, faster, let me out, I need you, she purred.

The girl was scraping and pounding at the wall. She waited for what seemed like forever when she heard a click and anticipated the wall opening.

"What the hell? What happened to you?" Cadence dropped her control and winced. She was caught! "Cadence!" he roared, "Stay out of her head! Oh god, baby, let's get you cleaned up."

"Derrik? Oh God, I'm bleeding!" the whore started to scream. Cadence couldn't help but laugh at the thought of what the girl had done to herself trying to get to her.

She listened as the screams turned to sharp sobs and Derrik uttered reassurances.

Light assaulted her eyes and Cadence turned her head against the harsh intrusion.

"Cadence, baby, look at me," came the voice she hated more than anything else on earth.

She tried to open her eyes only to have them burn with the light. She blinked several times then finally opened them and began to focus on the fuzzy form in front of her. Derrik's chiseled features slowly came into focus. His blue eyes were cold and hard as he waited patiently for her to come into awareness. She finally looked at him. His blond hair was braided over his shoulder and blood marred his crisp white shirt.

"Cadence, I love you and I'm doing this for your own good. Try and use the child that way again and I will punish you with another stake. Do you understand?" he said in a calm cool tone that reminded her of several conversations that they had had over the years, where his logic had always seemed to win out. She didn't answer she just stared at him. Did he really expect an answer?

"Cay, do you understand?" he asked more firmly. When she still didn't answer he grabbed her chin and squeezed.

"Yes, damn it! Let go!" she growled and pulled away. "Let me out, Derrik."

"Not yet. You hurt the child Cay. I've taught you better than that."

"Then at least let me feed, it hurts…" her words trailed off as she stifled a sob.

"I'm sorry Cay, you should have thought about that before you hurt the girl," he said then leaned forward and kissed her forehead.

"No, Derrick, no please!" she pled desperately as the door shut on her.

She pulled her hand back as it shut just before her toes. This time she freaked. The dark overwhelmed her and she began screaming and crying at the same time. It was pure and simple panic that took over. The closet began to close in, the dark consuming her body and fear took over. She felt a hand run over her body, then another. Then sharp claws tore down her back and she cried out in pain. More lacerated her thighs and torso. Cadence screamed as they assaulted her vulnerable body. She danced in place trying to move, to twist and to turn, anything to get away from their grizzly touch. She smelled her blood as it poured from the wounds and began to whimper when the claws finally receded. What were they? How did she have any blood left? Why wasn't she dead? She cried inside the wall, body aching and burning simultaneously.

When Cadence finished flipping out she noticed her body didn't burn where the claws had raked it. She raised one hand up and felt no blood on her body—well, no new blood anyway. She sighed and thought for a minute. Damn it! Derrik had done it again: he'd tricked her. There had been no claws! The fear had come directly from his mind. She banged her head against the wall at her stupidity. When would she ever learn? She knew he was powerful because he was an old vampire; she knew all this yet she had let him inside again, had let him tear her apart. If Cadence weren't careful she would succumb to his mind games and become a puppet again. She fumed standing there in the dark.

Suddenly sounds from the bedroom wafted out again. God how she hated him!

What did he think he was doing? She couldn't understand the fake love he claimed for these young people. But she'd seen it, twisted on his face like some hideous mask every time he brought a new one home. Gasping, she realized now that he really did believe it. Derrik really did think he loved them. It didn't make any sense whatsoever. The only reason she had played along with the games when she was younger was because she had deluded herself into believing she loved him, and she would have done anything to show him how much she had loved him. Anything! She had even taken to drinking the "children's" blood like he did *before* he turned her. How many diseases had she been exposed to? How many moral laws had been broken?

Bile rose up in the back of her throat as she thought of all she had done in the name of love. Twisted, sick, wrong love. It ate at her like acid as she began to see each and every face of every person he had brought home over the years, faces with names she couldn't remember—such beautiful and innocent faces.

Another thought struck her. What had he done with them? Once they had finished playing the games, what had he done with them? Were they alive some were? Had he kept them? Locked them away? Oh God, what had she done? What had she been a part of?

Cadenced winced again as the light assaulted her shuttered lids. Expecting Derrik, she gasped as a small frail figure came into view.

"I found you," the figure said and stared at her with eyes wide. Before Cadence could stop herself she snatched the girl by the neck and sliced into her throbbing pulse. Sweet blood rushed into her mouth as the girl began to struggle. She gulped quickly and prayed

Derrik wouldn't catch her feeding on his whore. As the blood filled her insides, the pain became a dull ache and she sighed against the girl's throat. The flow started to slow, but still Cadence drank. She pulled on her throat until the blood merely trickled from the twin wounds. As the last of the blood left the girl's body Cadence heard her heart stutter then stop. She pulled back in horror and dropped the limp girl to the floor. Now she looked at the angelic face and recognized it for who she was. The whore was dead. She cringed as she thought about the nickname she had given the young girl.

It was all very sad really and had she not been left in a wall to die, she would have probably felt really remorseful about killing the girl. She reached up and grabbed the stake in her hand—so much stronger now—and pulled. It came loose and she fell to the floor in a heap on the dead girl. Blood ran for a moment down her body, then trickled, then stopped and Cadence felt the tingle that accompanied healing. She moved her legs and pulled herself up on the wall. The feeling came back as she straitened her knees. She noticed a snore coming from down the hall. Quickly she shoved the dead girl in the wall and shut it tight. She inched down the hall until she reached the door.

A tall lanky young man with a mop of curls lay sprawled across the bed. She heard his heart as it beat strong inside his chest. She went to the bed and inhaled his scent. Her teeth lengthened in her mouth as she bent over and bit into him. The boy twitched at the action, but continued to doze. Cadence drank greedily at the sweet blood and the aches began disappearing with each passing mouthful. She stopped right before his heart stopped and watched as he took his last breath, the body twitching one final time. It didn't occur to her to feel any emotions for him—he was a nobody. She went to the bathroom and showered, cleansing the blood and stain from her body. She dressed in a pair of jeans and a dark blouse and then put on her favorite running shoes.

Somewhere between the shower and dressing she began to formulate a plan. She went to the garage and found the extra gasoline can. The plan included fire.

Cadence began to trail a line through the house, out the front door and onto the sidewalk. She had found a book of matches as she had walked through the house with the fuel as well as a large hunting knife. She wasn't sure where it had come from or why it was among Derrik's possessions, but it quickly became part of her plan. Her hand shook as she tried to light one small flimsy paper match. Her eyes began to tear and her shoulders shook as she tried again and again. Finally it struck and she cried out in relief. She tossed it at the gas and then ran as fast as she could. She heard the match hiss as it hit the gasoline and by the time she reached the road the house was a roaring inferno. Cadence watched it burn for a minute then retreated to the shadows of the trees to wait.

Cadence crept from tree to tree watching Derrik as he wailed and cursed her name. Her shoes soundless of the soft earth she peered through the low hanging limbs. When he didn't seem to notice her presence she began the walk toward him. Her teeth slid out, her vision sharpened and her pulse sped up, anticipating the coming fight. She slid the knife from the small of her back where she had tucked it into her jeans. It felt large and heavy in her hand. Cadence wrapped it tight in her fingers, the blade catching the firelight of the burning house. When she was directly behind Derrik she stopped, feet spread wide apart, right hand holding the knife out a little from her side, left hand balled into a fist.

"Get up you bastard," Cadence hissed between clenched teeth. She had seethed for hours and the anger that had grown sat like a ball of heat in her chest ready to explode. She watched his body still as the recognition settled over him. Derrik rose to his feet and slowly turned to face her. His face was streaked with bloody tears and he glared at her through swollen eyes.

"You killed them Cay. Why did you kill the children?" he accused.

"Shut up, you sick bastard. That whore deserved to die," she spat.

"No Cay, the children, they…they were in the basement, locked in their room, and you burnt the house down around them. They were trapped. Why did you kill my precious children?" he whispered in disbelief as his eyes searched her face.

She just stared at him. What was he saying? What children was he talking about?

"You're not making sense and I'm not in the mood to talk to you," she said raising the knife higher.

"But they were to be our family. I changed them, all the ones I brought you. I made them like us for us to love. They needed us and you killed them," he said his voice increasing in volume. Derrik's hands begin to ball into to fists and his fangs shot into view. "I have to punish you for this Cay. I can't let you hurt the children and go unpunished," his voice shook as his rage began to mount.

The total realization of what had happened to each innocent Derrik had brought to her struck her hard. She realized each and every single "victim" he'd brought home had been locked up in the soundproof basement of the mansion she'd burnt to the ground. Normally, such a savage realization would have bowled her off her feet—literally—but the enraged hatred within her pushed such thoughts away and forced her to meet the insane monster whom had tried making her into his own image.

Derrik stepped toward her and she held her ground. She was no longer afraid of him, of what he could do to her. Between one heartbeat and the next he was at her, hands around her throat and pushing her to the ground. Cadence brought the knife up and stabbed it into his side. He didn't so much as wince in pain, but he was growling deep in his throat and squeezing her neck. They hit the ground and her head connected with the gravel of the driveway. He barred his fangs and reached with his hands, one tangling in her hair. He jerked her head to the right. She fought and roared at him, her arms coming up in front of her with the knife still clutched firmly in her hand. The fresh scent of his blood filled the air as it spilled onto her chest.

Derrik's weight was heavy on her body, but she fought him as he went for her throat and instead he bit into her forearm. She screamed in pain and used the fisted knife to punch him in the jaw, then in the chest. He lost his hold on top of her and she scrambled to push him away. His hand still held her hair and she bent at the waist as she stood. He lunged from his knees aiming again for her neck and her pounding pulse. As the force and weight of his body shoved her back down, she pushed the cold steel blade between them, wedging it at his throat while grabbing the top of his head by the hair.

"Get the fuck off me, asshole," she growled. "Or I'll be holding your head above your fucking shoulders!"

His face turned to mild amusement as the blade pushed against his skin. He backed up as she sat forward and kept the knife trained on his throat.

"Cay, why are you doing this?" he asked, his voice taking on a honeyed timber that she knew was meant to soothe.

"I hate you and I hate what you've done to me. You're sick and I won't be like you…ever!" she shouted and leapt at him. Having gained the upper hand she landed on top of him and scrambled to pin his arms. He began to laugh deep in his chest, it rumbled out of his throat as some kind of maniacal roar that scared her.

"Shut up," she hissed and pressed the blade harder to his throat, this time drawing blood. He continued to laugh. Her fury exploded and her vision tinted red. She drew the hunting knife quick and hard across his throat. The skin popped open and blood ran down his neck. Derrik coughed and hands flew to his neck, his eyes wide.

Cadence drew the blade above her head and with both hands

plunged it into his chest. He roared and arched off the ground. She twisted then pulled it out to plunge it back in again. The blade dripped blood onto her hands and down her arms as she raised it for another strike. Arms fastened around her waist and pulled her back. She snarled and bit at the arms, fighting to get back to Derrik. She was in an absolute rage as she turned on her attacker and drove the knife into his gut—in her enraged state she didn't even notice who it was she'd just stabbed. She briefly saw him in her peripheral vision as he grunted and stumbled back. Whoever he was, he was gone. Cadence jumped back on Derrik as he writhed on the ground and she bit deeply into his throat. Then she pulled and tore it out, blood spurting over her face and chest. She plunged the knife again and Derrik screamed as flames began to engulf his body—the signs of an ancient vampire succumbing to final death. Cadence jumped off him and watched as he burned. The light from the flames danced eerily with the glow from the house.

She turned then on her would be attacker prepared to do battle again. When her eyes landed on the young innocent face of Eli she gasped.

"No!" he screamed as Derrik's body began to sizzle. He was on his feet and lunged at her, fangs barred. Cadence brought the knife up and sliced at him, easily cutting into him while evading his hands and fangs. He got a funny look on his face as he stopped in mid motion, then fell to the ground. His body went one way and his head went the other.

Cadence fell to her knees. She sobbed into her hands.

Cadence sat wrapped in her lover's arms, his soft skin warm against her cold body.

"Cadence can we do that again?" Eric asked in a small voice.

"Of course we can," she replied and pressed a kiss to his rosy lips. She nuzzled Eric's throat and licked his skin, tasting the salty texture on her tongue. Her teeth ached and she plunged them deep into his vein. Hot sweet blood rushed into her mouth and the boy sighed as she pulled from him. When she finished, she licked the wounds closed and pulled back to stare into his face.

Eric looked like an angel, dark curls hanging in his blue eyes, his cheeks flushed with their love making.

"I love you," he said. He was so sweet and innocent…so in need of someone to love him just as she had needed to be loved when Derrik first discovered her.

"I love you too, baby," she said as she thought about the years she'd spent alone since Derrik's death, years she had spent pondering his actions. One day, when she had met Jacob, it had all begun to make sense.

He had been dirty and ragged, hungry and bleeding, and he had needed her. And she had needed a family.

Derrik had been right all along, she thought. She eased from the bed as Eric fell asleep and headed for the hall. Still naked, she pressed the wall and it popped open. She pulled back the wall and leaned her head against it.

"How could you do this to me?" he whispered.

"You have to learn, Jacob. You can't hurt the children. I need you all, you're my family," she said with a shrug of her shoulders. Then she stepped forward a placed a light kiss on his forehead.

"Please let me out, I'm sorry… I'm so sorry Cadence," he begun to cry as she smiled and shut the door on him.

THE END

UNFAIR
By John Miller

I bled my soul until it was dry, and then I bled it some more. Cigarette smoke hung in stale air. The monitor glowed pasty against my skin. No one read what I'd written this year. No one would read what I'd just finished. I was fine with that. That's what I told myself. It bothered me on the deeper layers of my mind, those portions I was able to sweep beneath the rug of consciousness most the time. Eventually the angst poured out of me. I thought of God giving me an addiction to writing when I had no audience, of making a woman feel a deep heartfelt love for a man who wouldn't return it. Why did these things happen? I didn't know, but I would have my answers.

Someone knocked at the door. I smiled and checked my watch—nine o'clock. He was here. Giddy, I raced up the basement steps and let Pastor Percy inside.

"What seems to be the problem, son?" he asked after we said our hellos. "It's late for me, and I'm usually finishing the Sunday Sermon's final preparations by this time."

"I never thought of that, Pastor Percy," I returned with a smile. "I guess Saturday nights are busy times for men of the cloth."

He gave me a smile, but it was filled with worry as he glanced at his watch, an indication it was time to get this meeting going. I led him downstairs and he muttered something about cigarette smoke, but I ignored the comment. I led him into the basement room where my computer rested on a mahogany desk. The walls were baby-blue, and a bunk bed rested against the far wall. Dust littered the floor in small heaps the way hair does when no one's cleaned it, and I sat before the computer.

"This room could use a good dusting," he remarked while

sitting on the lower bunk bed. I smiled as I brought up the file. "Is this what you want me to see, Mike? A computer program? You called with such…urgency in your voice that I came almost immediately."

"It's all here, Pastor Percy," I told him while standing. "Have a seat."

I pulled the swivel chair back over the deep-blue carpeting and nodded toward the chair. He hesitated, then he shrugged his shoulders. His white hair was greased back like they did in the Fifties, but a few silver locks hung over his brow. I imagined him leaning over his Bible in some study at his house, preparing the message for the Faithful the following morning.

"Just read what I wrote," I told him eagerly. "I need an audience, pastor."

He smiled, nodded, then pulled the chair up and began reading. What I'd written wasn't my best work, to be sure, but it would get the point across. His face lost its color halfway through the story—that was when I knew I had him by the balls. The story was about a man who wrote…and wrote and wrote and wrote and nobody read what he wrote. The man decided he needed to know the answers as to why God would place such a burden upon him, to be addicted to writing yet have no audience. The man in the story thought of many things: women who loved men who never returned that love; soldiers on both sides of the battlefield praying to the same God for safety and victory; employees who hardly tried at their jobs getting promoted only because of social ties with their employers, while the hardest working employees never received promotions; people who wished for love living alone, and those who didn't care about love going through lovers as easily as models trying on clothes; the wicked rich getting richer while the poor got poorer. At the end of the story, my character called the local small town preacher and invited him into his home on Saturday night. There he interrogated the preacher to get the answers as to why life was so unfair. He tortured the preacher, then slowly killed him.

"This…is quite a story," he said at last while standing. "I hope you know I'm not the least bit worried."

He turned and faced me. I held a sledgehammer in my trembling hand. I had more tools in the metal closet resting against the wall. I would get my answers from God himself that night.

"Not the least bit worried…" his voice trailed off while looking at the hammer.

"I want answers," I told him flatly. "If you don't know the answers, consider life unfair. If your God won't save you, if he won't give you the answers I seek, then consider your end as unfair as my life has been…as unfair as anybody's life of shattered dreams."

He grinned and I hesitated. The strength in his ice-blue eyes unnerved me.

"What…what are you thinking?" I asked at last.

"That you're ready, my son," he said eerily.

He spoke Latin and shadows swept about my room. Wind gusted and blew folders open, stories I'd written and printed wafted in the air. An evil presence filled the room. Pastor Percy grinned.

"For thousands of years the Church, whether it be Catholic or Protestant, has led its followers," he told me as shadows solidified and held me against the wall. "The Church leads the People, guides them, and gives them spiritual nourishment when needed."

I tried to scream, but when I opened my mouth the shadows slid inside choking down my voice and filled me with dying terror. The shadows held me a full foot off the floor, and I could not free myself. Pastor Percy took the sledgehammer from my hand and stepped back. He poised himself ready to strike, the sledgehammer held like a baseball bat in a baseball player's hands. He took practice swings while he spoke.

"The Brotherhood took over the Church eons ago," he explained. "Through temptation, trickery and deception we destroyed the godly and deposited our brethren amidst the rulers of your Church. Over time we took over.

"I can see your spiritual progress has come along beautifully, son. You were ready to kill me for answers, weren't you?" His grin widened as he swung a practice swing. "The answer as to why life is unfair is simple: the Brotherhood rule humanity's petty lives."

With that spoken, he brought the sledgehammer against my skull crushing it. The crunching skull bones fractured and slit into my brain. My physical body died instantly, but my soul slid out of my body and hovered before him. Although incorporeal, he saw me and commanded the shadows still holding me captive to take me to hell. This is how I came to be here.

I sat in the swivel chair which was not at all unlike my own swivel chair sitting before the computer back in the basement of my house. Pastor Percy sat in that chair now, typing a new ending to my own story. That's what the demon sitting before me behind the large desk was explaining.

"Before you enter hell," Baalam explained with a sharp jutting finger black as coal, "Let me explain what is happening and will happen back on Earth. Pastor Percy is finishing your story even as we speak, and then he'll send it to a publisher. It will be accepted and sell around the world. Had you merely joined us, the Brotherhood, with our demons and converts on earth, you would have enjoyed this same success. Instead you prayed to a God we killed on a cross thousands of years ago.

"That is why the world is so unfair, Michael," the demon leered with a fanged smile. He leaned back in his chair and interlocked his fingers behind his blackened head. "We've been in control for a long, long time."

Next, they had me write my final moments on Earth, how I died, and how I came to hell. I had to use my own blood. It was unfair, but this is my story. They say to be careful for what you wish for—you just may get it. I wished for answers.

I got them.

Even now I hear the screams of the dead, a cacophony of blind pain and eternal torment interlocked in one universal scream of damnation. Soon my voice shall join that universal scream of damnation, and my torture shall continue eternal. I just wish sincerely that I hadn't sought answers to questions best left unsaid.

The End

Sparkles
By Kelly James

I couldn't snap the bitches neck with my cock imprisoned between her iron jaws lined with flesh ripping teeth. Sparkle's body rested half in the shower and half out, her front paws digging with vengeance at my thighs while her back feet scraped for purchase on wet tile of the tub's base.

I smacked helplessly at her narrow snout, but each successful swat brought fresh waves of agony from my bloody and torn dick. I'm sure I screamed, but Deb was still at work and the closest neighbor was a mere two miles away.

I was on my own.

Sparkles growled as she twisted and pulled on my member, her small black eyes staring up at me. She'd been waiting for this opportunity for awhile now, and I knew this fight would be the battle that ended our war.

I had to win, surrender wasn't an option.

I risked dismemberment and jerked backwards slamming myself against the shower wall. Even the rough drag across the tub's edge and a violent collision with the waterspout wasn't enough to convince the bitch to relinquish her grip.

My feet slid and I crashed hard on my ass on the slick floor banging my head on the soap tray on the way down. The stars filling my vision and the warm, thick sensation flowing from behind my ear barely registered in comparison to my mauled cock.

As a menagerie of shampoos, conditioners, and body washes rained down on my head from the broken shower caddy, I reflected on how I'd arrived at this painful conclusion.

Things went south when Deb brought the surprise gift home one windy day in March. Our home sits situated between endless fields of corn with the main pipeline to Columbus running through our front yard. The traffic is considerable considering our secluded locale, not at all suited for birthday puppies to roam.

I should make this clear; I did not want the fucking dog. Dogs are eating and shitting machines designed solely for purpose of destroying carpets or furniture or expensive things small enough to fit in their grinding jaws. I'm more of a cat man. Cats are self-sufficient and generally do not annoy on the level a newborn puppy.

Therefore, the little mutt shocked me when Deb presented her to me as a *gift*.

"What's this?" I asked as Deb handed me the box with the telltale holes poked in the top and the soft thumping emitting from inside which could only have been a tail wagging.

"Happy birthday, baby," her brown eyes danced with excitement as I held the shifting box.

I didn't want to open and have whatever critter spring on me, but there are some things a man must do. Accepting unwanted gifts from his significant other is one of them. I pulled the flap back and before I had a chance to register exactly what it was I saw, razor-like teeth bit into my thumb.

"Ouch," I quipped, withdrawing my hand. The pointy snout poked through the opening was undoubtedly canine.

"Isn't she cute?" Deb held both her hands under her chin, clasped together. I knew she hoped for a riveting sign of approval from me, but the best I could offer was a wary smile.

"She certainly is." I risked my fingers as I reached in and pulled the little dog out. I held her out at arms length and appraised her. She was pretty, for a mutt. Her entire back gleamed with soft black fur that took on a *gun barrel-blue* tint in the pre-spring sun.

Delicate light brown fur coated her underbelly, her snout, and framed her eyes. She looked kind of, like a Rottweiler crossed with a Beagle.

How that union happened, I didn't want to think about. The physics of it were just *wrong*.

"Well," Deb watched me with hopeful eyes. She wanted my approval, my appreciation.

I tried, but couldn't manage a convincing expression. "What about Ivan?"

"Ivan has claws. If Sparkles tries anything, Ivan will send her running with her tail tucked between her legs."

"Sparkles?"

Deb blushed. "I couldn't resist, she just *looks* like a Sparkles. If you want to change her name, that's fine with me."

I'm smart enough to know not to question a woman's judgment on such matters, besides Sparkles fit the puppy perfectly. Sparkles just didn't fit me.

"Do you like her?"

"She's great! I think Sparkles and I will be good friends." I lied. The puppy looked innocent enough, but I knew I'd spend countless hours outside trying to teach the dog to shit in the grass rather than our burber.

Time passed and Sparkles grew. Within three months, my puppy nearly tripled in size and weighed in at roughly forty-five pounds. She practiced regular teething on my shoes and sunglasses and fingers. Not to mention the extra expense in paper towels I had to buy to keep up with her puppy bombs she'd leave. I suspect *Bounty's* stock rose that spring.

The one thing I found most disturbing about Sparkles was her aversion to following me to the basement to watch me work. She refused to budge at the top of the stairs and if I tried to force her down, she'd growl and retreat to her cage in the bedroom. I suppose, if I'd been a wiser man, I would have took the hint.

I'm a novelist by day. I weave words of bullshit and lies send them off to some publisher on the East coast who turns my babble into a monthly check. I'm not a big moneymaker like Stephen King or Dean Koontz, but I get by well enough to not have the anchor of a *real* job hanging around my neck. A writer can ask for no more.

Writing my novels allows me time to concentrate on my ultimate goal. During the day, when Deb is working, I go to the basement and concentrate on my real work. The work God put me here to do. This, it seems, is where Sparkles and I disagree.

I have no doubts the dog isn't really a dog at all, but a Hellhound sent to stop God's work. She'll find I'm not easily deterred.

***

Day one with Sparkles started out innocently enough. I awoke at five, a full hour before Deb would rise. I put coffee on, took my shower, and started for the den to begin my day of weaving bullshit.

As I worked my way through the house in the dark—I leave the lights off in the mornings to allow Deb her extra hour of sleep— carrying a mug of Irish Cream diluted coffee, a pack of *Camel* cigarettes, and the daily edition of *The Columbus Dispatch*, I stepped in something mushy.

Hairball, my mind screamed and my stomach grew rebellious.

The only drawback to Ivan the cat was his ability to produce disgusting cocoon things of cat food and hair. I could live with that though; it wasn't like Ivan had a choice.

I continued. I'd clean the mess up later, but now, I had three thousand words I needed to bang out before noon if I wanted to stay ahead of that idiot hippy horror writer in White Rock for sheer volume of published work. It's the small things that keep me going.

I sat down in front of my computer, sat the coffee and newspaper off to the side, and stared at my reflection in the dark screen. This was a habit of mine, my moment of silence before the big game if you will. I looked genuinely creepy in the monitor's dead stare. The cigarette illuminated my features just enough to give my reflection a dusky pallor and the face looking back at me appeared dead or at the very least, dying.

I don't believe in premonitions or omens, but at the moment I thought those things about my reflection, I smelled an awful odor emitting from beneath the desk and heard a light *thumping* from across the room.

It didn't take me long to discover the source of the beastly smell. I flipped on the desk lamp and looked under the desk, everything looked kosher with the exception on my right foot—the one that had found the hairball.

Only I saw then it hadn't been a hairball at all. Between my big toe and the next piggy oozed a clod of brown matter I recognized instantly as shit. More properly, dog shit.

And the thumping I heard turned out to be the shit leaving culprit sitting in front of the door, wagging her tail.

I know now, day one was just a precursor for things to come.

***

Life went on mostly as it had before Sparkles. Deb seemed to be in a better mood coming home greeted by an excited puppy, jumping and wagging its tail, all for her. But for me, time did nothing to ease the transition of life with Sparkles.

Once Deb left for work, Sparkles went through some kind of metamorphic change. She ceased the playful puppy routine—I'm confident routine is exactly the right word—and shifted more towards the traditional demeanor of a villain. As soon as Deb's car started, shifted into reverse, and the sound of gravel crunching beneath the tires signifying her departure, Sparkle's tail became rigid and her playful eyes turned menacing.

She'd stand facing the door, her back to me, and turn a slow circle in my direction until she faced me full on; her head hung low and a hint of the razor teeth showing beneath a curled lip.

It was like that throughout winter. Sparkles and I played the little hate game everyday, but when I brought home my first subject of the winter for my *special* work in the basement, Sparkles became unhinged and tried to attack me.

Sparkles still wasn't big enough for the attack to register beyond annoying, but the hate and zest in the bitch's eyes seemed uncanny. I paused, watched the dog attack my pant leg a moment before a well-placed Reebok sent her against the wall with a yelp.

She still would not let up.

I managed to carry Lucy's unconscious body down the stairs with out falling, Sparkles barking and growling and gnawing at my leg the entire way. It is a wonder I didn't fall and break my neck.

"Will you fucking stop it!" I demanded, but Sparkles didn't obey.

I laid Lucy on my worktable and admired her shape for a moment. I couldn't enjoy my work with the constant yapping though, so I had to do something about Sparkles.

"Come on, girl. Let's go outside." I cooed trying to mask my anger as I knelt and extended my hands invitingly.

Sparkles calmed, regarded me with a twist of her pointy noggin, and stepped forward.

I should have known something was wrong by her tail not wagging, but as I've said, I'm not a dog person and I can't be expected to catch all the little tell-tale signs the mutt communicates. When Ivan is hungry, he meows, when he wants love, he rolls over. Simple gestures easily understood. Forgive the hell out of me if I don't speak dog.

Knelt before the little beast, I was in a position that left me vulnerable to her puppy teeth. Sparkles made full use of her advantage and locked onto the pinky and ring finger of my left hand.

I tried to jerk away, but my efforts only strengthened her grip, digging deeper into my flesh.

As the pain lit my hand up and I realized I wasn't getting loose without violence, I hit the dog repeatedly with my right fist. The agonized yelps emitting from Sparkles soothed me somewhat as if causing her pain eased my suffering somehow.

It didn't take long for my fist to convince Sparkles to relinquish her hold. Once free of my hand, she raced upstairs whining like a siren.

The low ceiling and dampness of the basement seemed suddenly to close in on me as I examined my bloody hand. Normally, blood didn't bother me, but I had never seen this much of mine to conclusively test the theory before. The edges of my vision began closing in. I knew I was about to faint, but the knowledge did little to prevent my collapse.

The last thought I had before I slumped unconscious to the floor was of Sparkles and the damage she could reap if she decided to make a return trip to the basement.

***

Sparkles hadn't come back though.

I awoke lying on the dirty floor with a headache and two screaming digits. As the grogginess of sleep faded, Lucy's memory struck my mind like a hammer. God, if she'd awakened while I was out and escaped—I didn't want to think of the ramifications of such a thing.

I pulled myself up to fast and a wave of dizziness forced me down again. Steadying myself against the block wall, I tried once more. I stood on shaky legs threatening to give out at any moment, but the relief I felt when I saw Lucy's unconscious body where I had left her washed through me like a cool breeze.

I looked at my watch, ten till six. I'd been out much to long and wouldn't have time to properly process Lucy. Anger reared its ugly head inside mine.

Fucking dog, Sparkles had effectively ruined my day.

I mentioned before, I make my way in this world by publishing bullshit and lies. I've also mentioned I serve a higher purpose than merely writing fiction. I work for God.

At least once a week I get messages from upon high—God's will in the form of dreams. God tells me things, things normal men aren't meant to know. He, rather than soil his holy hands, consummates his wishes through me.

God sends me a vision, a story, of a sinner near my hometown of White Rock. He relays the manner in which he wishes the sinner punished and I act as *God's hand*. Sometimes the almighty only wishes a sinner warned—he once had me beat a teenage boy with a cane pole and poke his eyes out for masturbating to internet porn. Other times God isn't so merciful, as in the case of lovely Lucy Spicelli.

Lucy had thought since her boyfriends eighteenth birthday fell on the same day as the senior prom, she'd give him an *extra* special birthday present.

God did not agree.

And now, here she was, laid out before me awaiting God's punishment. If it hadn't been for Sparkles—correction, Satan's pooch—Lucy would already be before the almighty pleading her case.

But Satan's hound fucked everything up. Deb would be home soon and I still had to clean and bandage my wounded hand, not to mention do something to keep Lucy quiet. I couldn't very well kill her outright—not after the sin she was going to commit before God and I intervened.

I held my hand in front of my face and inspected the damage. The last two fingers looked like bloody sausage links. I wanted to kill Sparkles, but explaining that to Deb would prove difficult.

I wrapped my mangled digits in the tail of my shirt and moved next to Lucy's vivacious body lying on the table.   She looked magnificent.   I desperately wanted to play, but such things would have to wait until the next day.

My basement had a room further down.   Its purpose was as a root cellar, but I used it as cold storage.   After I finished dishing out holy punishment, I'd place the remains in the root cellar until a convenient disposal option presented itself.   On any given day, I'd have three or four corpses lying in the cellar wrapped in individual tarps.

I checked Lucy's bonds again.   I tightened the knots holding her arms and legs in place.   I wondered if a gag would be appropriate. I doubted even her loudest screams could penetrate the recesses of both the cellar and the basement, but the question that begged an answer, am I willing to chance it.

No, I wasn't.

I decided to gag and blindfold her; the risk was just too great. If she couldn't see, she'd be less likely to start screaming and more likely to just lay and weep.

I made my way back upstairs.   Sparkles was nowhere in sight.

Good, I almost said aloud.   I didn't want to deal with her right then.   I had things to accomplish before Deb returned, and Sparkles would only hinder me.

***

"How was your day?"   Deb looked tired.   Her shoulders slumped as she sipped from her can of *Budweiser* and held the day's mail with the other.

"Fine, it looks as if yours wasn't though."   I tried to hide my bandaged hand to avoid the inevitable questions and the lies I would have to come up with explaining the wound.

Deb stopped off at Little Tony's and brought pizza home for dinner. I realized Sparkles wasn't bouncing around Deb—the dog acted as if Deb was the messiah whenever she got home.

Had I hurt her worse than I thought? Suddenly, the wound on my hand got a lot harder to explain. Deb would no doubt think I hurt Sparkles because of the bite. Of course she was right, but I don't plan on ever admitting to it.

Or to the reason Sparkles was upset to begin with.

I had to think fast, any second Deb would wonder why the dog wasn't accosting her. Several plausible lies raced through my mind, but lying to Deb required a little something extra. She has the ability to see through bullshit, especially mine.

Funny thing, Deb, I thought, *Sparkles and I were taking a walk and this big* Cujo *looking dog attacked us. Bit my fucking hand, but pummeled the shit out of Sparks!*

It's a lame lie, but the best I could come up with on such sh—

Sparkles nails clicking on the hardwood stopped me in mid thought. She rounded the corner from the living room at full puppy speed, and leaped at Deb.

The stress of her day fell from Deb's face. Her smile beamed.

"There's my girl! You been a good puppy today?"

Sparkles answered with a wagging tail and hand licks.

Man's best friend my ass, I thought as I put on a phony smile.

We ate dinner while we watched what remained of the six o'clock news. Sparkles lay in the floor beside Deb's feet nibbling on a bone. I watched her. I thought I had hurt her, but she showed no signs of pain. Disaster averted.

Deb got up, took my empty plate, and headed for the kitchen. Sparkles followed her.

I relaxed and focused on the TV. Jerry Revish was telling us about the latest missing girl—Kimberly Grogan. The police still had no leads, he said, but foul play was suspected.

I smiled. Foul play had been involved, but now Kimberly Grogan rested in my cellar. I suspected Lucy wouldn't make the news until the following day, maybe later. I enjoyed watching the local news report on my doings. I didn't worry about them finding too much out, God wouldn't allow his soldier to be caught.

Barking from the kitchen pulled me away from the TV. Sparkles was going ballistic about something.

"What's going on in there?"

"Sparkles is going off at the basement door. I think an animal might be down there." Deb replied, her voice loud to penetrate Sparkles barking.

Fear washed through me. Would Deb open the door to investigate? Would she follow the damn dog all the way to the cellar door?

Fucking Sparkles, I should've snapped her fucking neck!

I moved like angry lightning to the basement door.

"Don't open it!" I arrived just as Deb placed her hand on the knob. "It could be a raccoon, they can get vicious."

Deb pulled her hand away as if the doorknob crawled with snakes. Her face looked worried and unsure. She hated the old basement filled with its spiders and grime, and the thought of a rabid raccoon down there probably scared the hell out of her.

Sparkles continued yapping and jumping at the door.

"What are we going to do?" Deb sounded scared all right. I half expected her to lock herself in the bedroom until the situation calmed. She wasn't one much for frights.

"I'll take care of it, just keep Sparkles quiet."

Deb snatched up Sparkles—still barking, even in Deb's arms—and retreated to the living room.

My God works in mysterious way.

I decided to use the opportunity to check on Lucy.

The basement sounded normal, no human noises at all. I descended the steps slowly until I the found the old pull string mechanism for the light.

Yellow light flooded the gloom, but made the shadowy corners darker than they were before. I've always feared the shadows lurking in the basement, it would be only a matter of time before Satan sent a demon to try and interfere with my work. I have no doubts The Prince of Lies has far worse monsters at his disposal than Sparkles.

I worked my way across the grimy floor, staying always in the lights path, until I came to the cellar door. I leaned in close, my ear nearly touching the Oak planks, and listened.

I heard an occasional ruffling of the vinyl tarp, labored breathing, and best of all, whimpering.

I smiled.

I shouldn't have opened the door, but I couldn't resist. Lucy lay on her back, her eyes wide with terror looking up at me. The way her tears smeared her mascara excited me.

I suppressed my joy and forced a look of aghast on my face.

"Are you hurt," I whispered.

Lucy shook her head no, but it wasn't a convincing gesture.

"I'll try and get you out, but please, stay quiet until I can make sure it's safe. I don't want to get caught and end up in there with you. Do you understand?" I felt a sense of pride bubbling up in my chest as I rattled off the lies to the frightened girl. Sometimes my genius amazes even me. If this little ploy didn't keep Lucy quiet, nothing would. Not to mention the added bonus of her despair when she realized her only hope, was the one plunging a knife into her.

I returned upstairs and reported the raccoon must have made a quick getaway. Deb wouldn't sleep a wink if she thought the thing still lurked somewhere in the house. Lies such as that, I could slip past her, especially in her frightened state.

We retreated to the bedroom, fucked, and slept peacefully. I wasn't worried about Lucy trying to escape anymore and Sparkles was safely locked away in her crate—she wouldn't cease the yapping, so Deb even agreed to the imprisonment.

I felt accomplished and proud as I drifted off to sleep. My last thoughts of the day were of Lucy and how much fun I'd have punishing her tomorrow. Of course, Sparkles would have to be dealt with as well, but the mutt could wait until the morning.

***

Deb and I both overslept.

She spent less than a third of her usual time preening and brushing in the bathroom. She didn't even remember to release Sparkles from her cage before she rushed out the door with a quick peck on the cheek for me.

I stood on the back deck, coffee cup in one hand and waving bye to Deb with the other. I watched her taillights disappear behind the corn as she rounded the curve. I smiled as I turned my thoughts to Sparkles.

It's going to be a good day.

I went to my desk in the den and slid the drawer open. The previous summer, I had went with Deb's father to a Cleveland Indians game and at the souvenir booth I purchased a replica bat. The bat was eighteen inches long and featured the Indians logo on it, it would make a perfect weapon which to bludgeon Sparkles to death.

I heard Sparkles rattling her cage; undoubtedly, the mutt had to piss.

I set my coffee cup down on the desk and started for the guest bedroom where Sparkles waited. I whistled as I walked. Why not, I was in a good mood.

As I stepped through the doorway, Sparkles started growling.

I smiled.

As I opened her cage, I took precautions against her vicious teeth. I stood behind the small door, making Sparkles have to circle around to get at me, leaving her collar exposed and easy to grab.

Once I had her collar, I twisted it hard. Sparkles gagged and tried to growl, but her attempts quickly turned to whimpers. I could simply twist her collar until she died of asphyxiation, but what fun was there in that?

Sparkles kicked and thrashed against me, but for all her efforts, she was still just a little dog. I started with her ribcage. Nothing takes the fight out of you quicker than your breath knocked out.

I felt righteous, almost god-like as I swung the bat into Sparkles' ribs. She screamed in high pitch wails, but with each stroke of my bat, her fervor eased. I continued pounding until she hung limp and motionless.

I dropped her to the floor as I knelt down to look in her demonic eyes, which twitched frantically. I'm not sure if dogs can cry, but I fancied seeing tears of pain and fear bubbling at the corners of her pretty browns.

"Satan's power is of no avail in the face of God's will, demon," I gloated, patting the bat against my hand. "Your dark master has failed you," with that, I commenced beating Sparkles' skull with the bat. She twitched and squirmed and whimpered, but eventually, a satisfying *thunk* ceased her struggles for good.

Her tongue lolled from the side of her mouth, blood oozing from every orifice on her body.

Sparkles was dead.

I carried her dripping body to the front porch, laid her down on the swing, and then trotted out to the mailbox. From the mailbox, I could see far in both directions, nothing was coming.

I raced back to the porch, collected her corpse, and unceremoniously tossed her to the center of the road.

I'd came up with a perfect plan, requiring no explanations to Deb, other than how she slipped from her leash and darted off into traffic. Nothing I could do. As I trotted back to the house I could hear a semi approaching. I felt proud of my accomplishment and my mind was already racing about the things I could do with Lucy in the basement now.

First things first though, I couldn't do God's work covered in Satan's filth.

***

And that is the story of how I ended up knocked silly in the shower with a zombie pooch gnawing on my manhood.

Sitting down against the back of the tub, dazed, Sparkles released her hold on my cock and immediately launched her maw at my throat.

My hands were to slow to stop her, and I screamed as I felt the razor like teeth shred the tender flesh of my neck. But worse than the impending death at the mouth of Sparkles, was the visions I saw in my mind as blood from my jugular flowed across my chest.

The visions were of the same type I received from God, only now I saw them from Sparkles perception and my blood ran cold as I realized my grave error.

It wasn't God who'd spoke to me, ordered me to kill all those people. And I wasn't the hand of God after all. Nor was Sparkles a Hellhound. I'd been deceived by the great deceiver, and willingly, I'd carried out Satan's wishes.

As the light dimmed in my vision, I felt an odd sense of irony. How funny is it that *I* should perish at the real Hand of God?

The End

Connect the Dots
(Part two)
By Alexzan Burton

Now that you've been used by us
Abused by us
Terrified and mused by us,

Your nightmares won't subside
Hold your eyes open wide

Watch the shadows on the wall
Shifting eyes on the doll

Cowering in the corner
The lightening reveals

Your murder.

Now your spattered blood adds
To our collection of

Connected dots